Greet the Dawn

Greet the Dawn

stories

Janet Lindquist Black

World Inside Press
New York 2020

Cover art by Janet Black
Cover and interior design by Tabitha Lahr

ISBN: 978-1-7328462-3-4
E-ISBN: 978-1-7328462-4-1

For Reed and Jenny, Damian and Sylvia.

When you wake . . .

thank the universe for another day.

Contents

A Liberal Education ✦ 1

Poika: 1929 ✦ 17

Suvetar ✦ 35

Loyal Opposites ✦ 43

The Gift ✦ 61

The Macaw ✦ 77

The Music Collection ✦ 85

Anticipation ✦ 97

Notes ✦ 115

A Liberal Education

My sister and I made the decision to send Mother to school. She'd had a childhood full of experience, none of it quite right for her future. She had helped her father make cellar wine until he left during the flood of '27, a night the river turned black and charged against them, almost drowned them at the supper table, and cleared out all the wine below, so that her father left no trace. For years thereafter, when she slept, a hand came and held Mother's fingers gently.

By age eight, she cleaned their two-family house from top to bottom in a single day while keeping an eye on five younger ones and cooking for Mimay in bed. She thought nothing of going out behind the house to catch frogs by the dozen, to fry their severed athletic legs for supper. Mimay did not believe in school for her children. In spring Mother spent most days with her sister skillfully leaping the log jams which crowded at the bend in the Androscoggin just below the bedroom window.

But none of this amounted to useful knowledge. As an adult, her spelling was terrible, and she was very shy with numbers. Even simple addition caused her to feel like a fool. When she reviewed the weekly grocery columns with the delivery boy waiting, he took the pencil from behind his ear and thumped the kitchen table. That impatient drumming of the eraser on the oilcloth further disturbed her frail ability to concentrate. We thought her headaches must arise from such vexing lack of command. It was too much that, even before the grocery boy, Mother should feel deficient.

Daphne and I chose the fifth grade for Mother, that point in our own school careers at which we left her behind. We also thought the fifth grade significant in our making, a suitable point for her to begin recovering what education and experience was not afforded by her own working life. She could sit inconspicuously beside Blaise Angevine, among the tallest pupils in the farthest row. Although we had done plenty of complaining about Sister Gabrielle-Marie, in retrospect much was learned from her tough-minded stress on mathematical discipline and attacks on idleness. It wasn't our intention just to be hard on Mother by asking her to undergo our past. But the hand of her sleep guided her like quiet religion, and assured her that life was small and comprehensible. She slept like the eternal dragonfly ensconced among water lily petals, as if calm ponds had separated from the river's rills. But in waking hours, she dragged defeated wings, and we emphasized the danger of confining herself to one little house that could be blown in by wind.

For her first school day, we made her resemble herself in her finest moment. Daphne found the brown gabardine suit with shoulder pads and the ivory crepe blouse with the supple catenary of jet sequins at the throat. She'd been photographed smiling in the outfit as she left the courtroom in 1943, having obtained over-time pay for the whole Friday swing-shift at the munitions plant. We never again saw her looking so inspired. She didn't want to wear the suit; she'd been rain-spattered in it on her wedding day and maintained that reviving times long gone invited insomniac spirits of ancestors. She also warned us again about contrived appearances being as subject to merciless drenching as bright summer afternoons.

Somehow the success of '43 led nowhere. As if in that victory she had passed for all times the test for survival, she had put away the gabardine suit until her wedding and returned to dwelling quietly and capably beside the river. Perhaps it was then that her face resolved itself into the shadowed philosophical contours of one who refuses to see anything not available to her. We tried now to bring back those fired moments of her former faith in something, all of which occurred before the Twister of '44, which finally left her family homeless, the bathtub standing alone in the field gripping the earth with ball-claw feet. Almost like lightning herself, she had married the sailor setting off for war. Though she worked in the plant until the war ended and her grinder spindle actually halted, they were all laid off after that, and in a way she seemed to retire.

On her first day of school, I walked her to the corner. We stood in the damp sunlight waiting for the school bus. I felt helpless thinking she seemed so unable to be recharged; it is because of something she has refused.

At the end of that first day, we three met at Howard Johnson's. She seemed happy enough going on with the waitress about the lopsided view one acquires of people by dealing with their hungry aspect. But we noticed the inattentive way she kept setting her fork against her poundcake, dislodging raisins and making crumbs. She talked about the picture story of Millet's *L'Angelus* they had pasted in their notebooks that day, but all the while letting us gather up her inconclusive sighs. The pungency of lemon wedges steamed up from our tea cups, and Mother folded her Salada label infinitesimally while she talked. Finally, when pushed, Mother admitted to feeling that everything went the way of the dog.

Florette, who had supposedly been so splendid in Mother's youth, had shed all loyalty when Mother married. The animal turned lazy and fat, started lying around the house, stealing food. Every now and then, Mother gathered the sneak by the ankles and flung her out the front door. But like bad luck, the dog came back whining, and Mother swore she thrived only because of fond memories of her own unencumbered teens as an arena star on roller skates, when the dog was faithful and spunky. Daphne paid the waitress who seemed, by the slant of her mouth, to agree with Mother generally. As we left the cushioned booth, Daphne and I were shocked to see on all our plates the same neat pile of rejected raisins.

Mother entered the parking lot first, leaving the swinging glass door behind in Daphne's hand: "All you have to do is live long enough," Mother said, "and everything hangs on and becomes annoying, like your father's swimming ear." Until that moment, we had frankly forgotten about Father, working at home now because of a slack period in the shop.

Next morning, Mother gave a hint of possible progress in school which encouraged us even about Father. Waiting at the corner, she remarked how the sunlight seemed to accompany the bus when it carried her away. We thought the remark positive because it presented a contrast to her usual resigned shutting away of morning when we all went off all those years leaving her home behind the door.

The next day we sent Father too. He had lacked the proper socialization, growing up an only child in that part of town full of white houses with drawn shades and Sundays which were pale blue and Protestant. He had been one of those peculiar farm children whom teachers can never induce to speak. In any case, the Navy had done more for Father than had school; he had even been photographed passing through New York once. We chose for him that same dark sailor uniform, and he looked tall and lean like a teen-aged fashion model, just as he looked in that Spring issue of *Modern Miss* in 1945.

We had always been proud of the way Father handled himself. Equally dazzled by foreign ports but more thoughtful about the future than his friends, he had not been stamped all over with indelible tattoos. Yet, like our mother, he had always seemed unfinished in the personal sense. We worried in different ways about Father. Though he is very gifted with numbers, he does not like the nuns. My sister and I chose not to fret about our parents while they were gone, and instead began the spring cleaning. We washed the odd pieces of Claxton ware, the soup tureen and cake plate on a stem which were dusty from lack of use. They had been Duz detergent bonus items and were the reason we bought the china closet. We cleaned the china closet too.

Then we laundered Mother's homemade slipcovers, and their superb crimson Shirley poppies did not fade as we had feared, but looked even more expansive, actually exultant, hanging outside on the line. After that, we set out the gladiola bulbs and gave the lawn its first close spring cutting with the hand mower. In all our busyness, we forgot to notice the day passing and were surprised to see them suddenly coming up the driveway.

Mother had the stubborn look of someone who will separate the raisins from her poundcake. Mother does not accept the universe. But there is the suggestion in her face, as difficult to see as the spot on her dark iris, the she might really care about something which she grows hopeless of imagining. Beside her, Father stood smiling. He has perfect teeth like all the Swedish farmboys. For a moment, we were surprised by that picture of them together. Mother still looked so neat and musical but vulnerable next to Father; her handbag nestled in the crook of her arm like something hurt. Father's happiness seemed so clear and blond and filled with future; his whole tall, large-boned body like a figurine poured from milk

As we expected, it was Mother who proved to have more problems in school. After the first two weeks she was already failing Math, and the French was European, not at all what she grew up speaking at home. For evenings on end she merely plinked at the piano waiting to watch Arthur Godfrey, Milton

Berle, Fulton Sheen, or Lucy, depending on the night. Then she put herself to bed like someone sick and spent hours escaping into analgesic sleep.

One night she awoke too soon, and found that the hand on hers was covered with sores and stiff, spiny bristles, and for the first time she experienced the abducting reach of a troubled ancestor. She threw words in English at it, for in all their generations up in Bellows Falls, having fought in every American war, they were never comfortable with the English language. Like someone dangerously unprotected, she rushed out next morning and joined the choir. A voice was deemed a meaningful offering, a living assertion against a menacing ancestor, to bite back any spirit which might have been sapped away. We thought the choir was wonderful, but an even further distraction from essential learning, without which she could be further misled.

Father's problems were less obvious. He didn't much enjoy singing in the choir, but mainly because he was bewildered by the chapel. Nevertheless, he loved his special math class for which only four had been selected, and it was taught by a Brother Boucher who traveled all the way from Holy Cross every afternoon. Father enjoyed the long, drawn-out problems which required the special craft of logic at which he was so adept, and Brother Boucher never mentioned religion. But it turned out that Father got along with everyone. Sister Gabrielle-Marie played baseball. She had a strong pitching arm and spent all recess and lunch hour on the boys' side.

Things went that way for a while. Father returned home each day and sat eagerly down to his homework, his slide rule and T-square laid out like chessmen on the green plaid oilcloth. But Mother had been frightened into relentless devotion at the piano; the purity of music was spiritually protective, and she held her voice in constant song. Father tried but failed to reach her with firm reason, and her math scribblings were done so carelessly even he was moved to pronounce the sheaf from her notebook not worthy of use as toilet paper. But she persisted in the *Agnus Dei* and *Panis Angelicus*, while Florette lay with her nose almost under the foot pedals and we sat listening. Mother's bass clef is made up of chords because she does not read music, but her right hand perfectly reproduces the treble.

When Good Friday came, Mother seemed temporarily to stop suffering from religion. They had shown a movie that afternoon in the auditorium, for which Father's math class was canceled. It was *Bernadette of Lourdes*. Mother enjoyed revelations of holy personalities and thought Pier Angeli acted the young saint to French perfection. She was happier now because school-work was less emphasized during Lent when everyone was busy seeking plenary indulgences, getting ashes, doing stations, and receiving communion daily. She spent more time in the choir and protected her hands in sleep by clinging to the vial of holy water brought from Lourdes by her hairdresser.

But Father was uncomfortable during religious times. He grew quieter and took on a little of his old disheveled look when his limp hair rises like agitated plumage. He started going back to the cellar at night to make bushings for drill jigs on his lathe. He made them in lots of five thousand and sold them to the customer for twenty cents apiece.

Well after two one morning, my sister and I finally waded through the ankle-deep steel chips to ask him what he thought about his future. We were entering a post-industrial era, we said, and was he going to keep tooling around with machines. He was wearing his plano lenses and spectacles gave his eyes an orbed, worried look. There was just enough room between the dangling light bulb and the rotating block for him to guide the honing bit against the tool. We spoke above the pitch of that cutting instrument which rose in its high-speed precision to a delicate wail. Father only smiled at our concern.

He said work was all that he needed, that his work made him happy and he had to force himself to quit at two AM. To us that statement revealed the first solid corner of the dangerous secret wall he was building to replace discarded hope. We couldn't disagree about happiness, but we asked if he had a plan to insure himself of a continually active mind. We recommended that he grow into the liberal arts and gain new friends, not go riding off every day for thirty-odd years with the same crowd from grade school in gray work outfits with lunch boxes and beaked shop caps, all heading into the sunrise. But he just laughed and made a vulgar joke. At the point when we were about to go away mad, he opened up the casing over the gear box and revealed with obvious pride eight perfectly meshed gears, which provided thirty-two variable speeds for cutting the stock into bushings. Of course, we understood, but we spoke about responsibility for taking care of oneself, about knowing when one is too good for something. Finally, without being insulting, we simply pointed out that a submarine heading toward Okinawa from Subic Bay might not have been the best place to be back in 1945.

Next day we went down to the cellar and put up wallpaper above the workbench, bright red with yellow stars, and we polished the grip vise and the soldering vise, and oiled the milling machine. Then we scrubbed the tool chest free of its oil, dust, and steel chip film, and treated the wood so the grain glowed like the ease of our accusations. After that we vacuumed the odd-sized, velvet-lined drawers, replacing the micrometers and calipers exactly as they were, and the chest stood like a splendid little military subordinate with polished mounts and handles so that Father could really feel himself boss. After lunch we went back and washed the cellar window up above the light bulb, since outside grew the mountain laurel which was bursting up there in spring like pink-streaked popcorn.

In the meantime, the season seemed to favor Mother. After Easter she became involved in the May Procession and was given the *Regina Coeli* solo. The act of public prayer song to the Queen of Heaven invited the interest of yet another ancestor, but one who had attained wisdom beyond the grave. If such a progenitor existed, it must find the soloist and guide her searching song.

This set two of them battling for Mother's soul.

Gathering for the challenge all the willing scraps of her being, every morning she sat at the piano. Father had barely endured Lent until Easter. His homework required so little of him, he finished it on the bus, and Brother Boucher missed Friday advanced math class now because of religious obligations. Father continued nightly on the lathe until he drove us crazy, but he truly missed his homework, and there was nothing we could do Then, no sooner did they finish Easter and his full schedule resumed that Father had a personal setback.

It seemed that Sister Gabrielle-Marie, while flying into home plate, had had the veil of her habit removed by the wind. Father isn't usually upset by details, but Sister's hair was clipped so close to the bones of her skull that she resembled a prisoner of war, and she also had the look of a newborn, and somehow in the surprise of that combination Father suddenly recognized what he thought was the immense mistake in her conviction about her life, as with children who run away: the Navy was full of them. Aroused to protectiveness he could not give her, he rethought the sobering episodes of submarine warfare after leaving New London, but he could bring none of it to Sister's situation; she would only smile and listen, and never recognize herself. He pitied her suddenly, teaching religion to rowdy misfits.

Then, just when Father realized how uncertain he was about everything, Brother Boucher, in the middle of introducing calculus, having so fully gained Father's trust, had suddenly likened first derivatives to Protestants, who may with superior goodness attain only life forever in limbo. "Unless they undergo integration," he said, "like conversion, and become realized in the formula, they do not even get back to their origins, or ever gain sight of God." He pointed out that there was nothing painful in limbo, depicted it as happy and comfortable, almost blankety for the Protestants. But the glimpse of God was Eternity, he said, was lasting love, the answer to everything, and life forever in limbo was not Eternity in the least. Father wasn't even Protestant; he'd never had any religion at all. The remark depressed him, coming from a mathematician.

But we were all so consumed by Mother's rite of redemption that we didn't even see Father disappear until we found his plano lenses on the lawn. In the meantime, every evening mother reproduced the whole gradual from morning mass. She sat straight-backed at the piano and searched for sounds planted in her mind. Her eyes had unusual brightness, and everything about her expressed perfectly the life of music. If her performance at the May Procession lacked perfection, she relinquished that chance of learning the deepest wish within herself. Finally, in practice, her *Regina Coeli* was splendid, and she said keeping musically attuned made nothing of the chore of daily Mass. She worked on the length of her notes and breathing details right up to the last hours.

Then, too late, she realized she had completely forgotten to consider the subject of appropriate dress. White patent flats were required, and Mother panicked when she found out late the night before. She had no light-colored shoes at all, and high heels were not appropriate for the fifth grade. It was so late, the stores had long since closed, and for all her careful planning she had forgotten to calculate that one monumental detail. She plopped dispiritedly into the armchair, into the encouraging lap of a bursting Shirley poppy. Without shoes she could not sing, she said. It was the same difficulty she had with math. Her careless neglect of detail accounted for her failure in school, and she reminded us how hopeless her actual school situation was. She had even been warned by Sister Principal of a chip on her shoulder.

Late that night, amidst junk in the attic, we found a pair of flats my sister wore in about the fifth grade. They were not white but black: they did not quite fit Mother, but for the few hours of the May Procession she could curl her toes. they also had enormous holes in the bottom right out to the edge of the soles. Daphne must have had a walking mania, or perhaps the shoes were from a heavily mortgaged time. Mother was very clever. She drew from an unadmitted part of her youth working in the Hudson Shoe Factory, in fact, cementing soles to shoes.

In the cellar, as if from a dream, she reclaimed our ancient kitchen linoleum from under the workbench. It had a blue background with red squares surrounded by white ones, and yellow squares off-center in the squared arrangements. Father had picked it out. It still bore the footmarks of the old Frigidaire which stood by the back door, one of the first things our family owned; it predated the Crosby on which we watched Milton Berle; it predated the Nash and the Electrolux, and may even have predated Daphne.

We hoisted a huge flush door across the set tubs because Mother shared her side of the workshop with the washing machine. Though Daphne and I had not yet gotten to the laundry, Mother was used to picking her way among shifting dunes of light- or dark-colored dirty clothes. Then Mother placed the shoes against the linoleum and with a flattened carpenter's pencil, outlined perfect soles. With the scimitar-shaped linoleum knife, she carved them deftly and carefully, which seemed to take a few hours. She kept wondering, she said, who among the generations up in Bellows Falls would turn up to extend the hand of salvation. Frankly she doubted if anyone among them was so inspired.

It was after midnight when she placed one shoe in the grip vise and the other in the soldering vise so that their cement could dry. That was when we missed Father. Where was he if not working on the lathe? We told Mother not to stop, to get the shoes painted white so they could have time to dry. Then Daphne and

I went out with the flashlight searching every bush and tree, until our light suddenly depicted the plano lenses perched on the velvet lawn like a defiant mosquito with enlarged golden legs and empty, flat, glass eyes, suggesting a search renounced.

Father was not in the garage, nor within calling distance. He had not taken the car, it glowed in the unctuous moonlight with large probing headlights like a monster full of gumption but unfavored by heaven. Daphne folded up the lenses, cool and dripping dew, and carried them in her hand. We lamented how it was especially wrong for people to be insensitive to Father, who had already been so disappointed by pettiness and small, unkind dissuasions of anyone trying to improve. Had we now made his life impossible sending him to school? Perhaps we should not bother ourselves being such busybodies.

It was almost sunrise when we trudged across Comtois's field and found him night-fishing in a runoff of the Androscoggin as happy as one who has recovered youth. His pail was full of fish and moonlight. We were speechless beyond forgiveness, though embarrassed when he reminded us about the prize trout of all our childhood springs, a fact we remembered very little anymore. We could hardly convince him it was not the fishing, but his lack of cooperation with an effort just to fit him better for a changing world. He reminded us again of his superior luck, having missed Coconut Grove the night of the fire. In the pail stirred the vigor of his allegiance to life as he knew it and felt most comfortable. The bounty of their childhood river was reliable and caused no suffering. We told him that we knew what Brother Boucher meant in his imprecise way about limbo. We asked if he had come to think all personal growth had ended, that his final colors had set and he had to live life out like the permanent tattoo. But Father would hear no more.

Daphne and I admitted walking home that the two of them were a lot of trouble. Father was basically a survivor of sorts, and perhaps trying to save Mother now was like trying to replant a tree uprooted by wind. For all the effort it was clear Mother was perfectly comfortable unenlightened and could not accept the penalties involved in growing. Why should she have to enlarge her future now? The present carried on like the large, lazy river, which turns violent only in extreme weather but mostly lets itself quietly by, reliable and undisturbing as the limbo of Brother Boucher. We could let her go on, as always, terrified that cyclones might bear away pieces of her life, family spooks competing for her slumbering hand. We thought we should just go back to Boston after the May Procession. But we still thought the May Procession a promising opportunity for Mother: one could see just by looking at her how little attention she'd received growing up.

Of course, the way the procession went was entirely in character. Mother, one of the tallest in her class, was placed to the rear, a disappointing position in itself. But they marched in threes, and the girl to her left was enormously fat, while the girl to her right was taller. Her shoes failed completely. The linoleum was too heavy and each step drew the shoe off her heel. She tried several elastics and set out with each whole foot and shoe embraced by a row of rubber bands all of which snapped in succession, and while she sang, dwarfed by her companions, her shoes had to be budged along the ground by the toes. When large, wet drops landed from the sky, appearing to make holes in her gabardine suit, her voice continued courageously until thunder dominated and everyone cleared out quickly in the middle of her pure sounding *meruisti portare*. She finished the song. But she refused to return to school, and we acquiesced to general defeat and all went out to Chin's Village and ate our fill of lobster fried rice.

We left them home like the worn pajamas that wrapped around our heads as we passed under the clothesline, happy with the mere air. We traveled and returned to our friends in Boston and lived happily and adventurously until years were gone. We only spoke occasionally. They called once to tell us they were preparing to die by giving away their furniture; and once again, it seemed, to say that our children were vagabonds let run in dirty, busy streets. Knowing they were content and that barring extremes of weather, nothing bad ever happened to them, we seemed to grow apart.

Daphne visited once on a holiday. To replace Florette who had died, she brought them a little mutt named Fidel left behind by a lover. They instantly adored him; they found dogs easy, and Daphne said she was not sure they even noticed when she left. Otherwise we did not go back. Our past seemed locked there, with them locked in it, and we guessed that they might have taken to bickering at night, which seems to happen to people whose lives shrink and settle.

Then, just before Daphne moved to San Francisco, we decided to see them. We called to tell Mother we were coming the next day, and do not know how she failed to tell Father. Perhaps to one another they have grown entirely mute with familiarity. When we arrived, the car was gone and no one was home. It was Saturday, Father should have been there unless he was working overtime. We guessed rightly that Mother must have gone in the car to do errands, we had stated no specific time of arrival. While waiting we set out for Comtois's field.

We could see the wild blackberry bushes singing up the mountainside, and we stopped by the great mossy creek at the edge of the field with two planks crossing like ancient grandmother sleigh tracks leading to the worn logging road in the forest. Here we learned the color green, we said; it sucked and gurgled around us while the lush branches above made us dizzy. The land was beautifully farm worn, full of all our summers as children, and things so basic we have given up.

Then, in the distance, we saw a man bending. He didn't look like Father, a little too elbowed and sharp, but mostly hidden by tall winter rye. It was the patch that Comtois liked us to cultivate, although we couldn't keep up with it every year. It was where

Daphne and I recited the *Angelus* once after a Friday afternoon movie about a saint; we were praying for a vision which never came to Mother. We were surprised when the man straightened, his head clearing the horizon so that even at that distance the sky seemed to peer through his eyes.

Perhaps Father ruined his perfect vision working such late nights on the lathe. Or maybe we have changed quite a bit ourselves. In any case, he didn't recognize us as we charged toward him, and we caused a most surprising reaction. He ran away—actually threw the hoe across his shoulder and made great panicky, awkward strides in no clear direction. What a terror ran through us. Then we noticed Fidel there, and Daphne stepped forward to extend her hand. But the little dog started and jumped suspiciously away and turned to run behind his master. We bolted after them, feet sinking in the fertile tilth across the seeming sea of our sunlit years.

Father turned quickly when he heard our voices calling, and, as if eclipsing a dream vision in rapid reverse, the friendly smile of innocence swarmed his boyish face. In that act of relaxing, his body transformed from a scarecrow configuration to that of the loose-jointed young swabby in uniform, the way we have always held him in our minds. In spite of what had now been irreparably revealed, we were happy to claim him, to show him we were not strangers, but, of course, we were. Like children, we wanted our mother and father. How sad the way we had to leave them standing questioning the sky where we had gone. Mother waited in the driveway with arms full of groceries, focused and friendly, as if awakening us on one of our earliest mornings for what we had to begin.

Published in *The Kenyon Review*. Volume III. Number 3. Summer 1981.

One of 100 Distinguished Short Stories of the Year 1981—in THE BEST AMERICAN SHORT STORIES 1982.

Poika: 1929

A FRIGHTENED BOY SAW AN INTRUDER at his father's door.

It was a Monday night in November, and Poika sat warming himself beside the Glenwood stove. He was the first to see Kaukanen come up the dirt road, throw open the front door, and stomp into the kitchen with mud flying from his feet. His boots shook the sturdy floorboards of the house, a squat, single story built by the boy's father not quite six years ago. Kaukanen came, knowing Aiti Karjalainen had forbidden him under her roof. But she was home only Thursdays now, and Kaukanen had chosen another night to come brandishing the whiskey bottle before the face of Karjalainen himself.

In the stove, charred bits of pine hissed and popped, settling to the cast iron bottom, resounding throughout the whole front room. The men were there, and Poika watched them with his lower back pressed against the wall. His forearms dangled from his knees, his left hand dressed with handkerchiefs blood-soaked at the crotch between the thumb and finger. His eyes were full of his father now, though he had not been able to look at him since Karjalainen took the knife away and hid it that morning. He thought his father was going to make a clean sweep of the shouting lumberman, as he had done long ago with the crazed Indian in the same kitchen. But Karjalainen hardly looked up from his cards.

"Mine whiskey been stolen," Kaukanen growled in English, not Finnish, making pouring motions to show how little whiskey was left in the bottle. "tooks me whole las' Sunday to hide diss pottle," he voiced his major preoccupation, and raised the flask as if to strike.

Poika thought this was like the time the Indian came threatening. He waited for his father to get up. Karjalainen remained unmoved, sitting at the table, guzzling his beer without answering.

Kaukanen clenched his huge free hand. "I'm used to get mine whiskey when I gonna want dem."

Karjalainen shifted his frame in a series of bored positions.

Kaukanen's puffed face was red. "I gut pour it in dog shit from now on? Piss in it? Kip mine neighbors hell away?" Sweat dropped to the floor. A chair fell over.

Then Karjalainen spoke gutturally through two absent teeth. "Marija tek it."

The boy heard. 'Now it comes,' he thought.

Kaukanen's cheeks fell, and the shocked colorless flesh spilled out from under his chin. Marija had been his mother. Long dead, she followed him from his boyhood on the other side of the Arctic, across the sea to Massachusetts, with the whipping chain secure on her wrist. Her footprints still appeared in his barnyard snow on windless nights, sudden rents were torn in his chicken wire fences, and once there were chain marks deeply gouged in the bark of a tree, a black birch that he never found again. Kaukanen, the Russian-Finn from Karelia, was quivering bear meat. His round head was hairless, his eyelashes without color, his eyebrows too faint to be seen.

"Diss, you home, gonna be roon py fire when you gut dem eyes iss close," he yelled as a final threat. Poika thought his father would surely go after Kaukanen now.

But Karjalainen simply lay the King of Diamonds on the Queen, and swept up the suit in his right hand.

KAUKANEN'S QUARREL HAD ANCIENT ROOTS in Arctic superstition. He hid his liquor from the same shadowy visions that bedeviled the icy tundra and the Finnish forests of his past. There, the silent darkness lay unbroken everywhere for half the year, reawakening the winter madness of suspicion that was only made bearable by drink. The people brought the gloom of centuries across the sea. Even in secluded New England lumber towns, a Finn secretly felt the disquieting memory of the still, hibernal North.

Poika knew something of his people. He knew about the woodsmen of old songs and stories, who made the madness their own, and laughed in solitude when they were old and spoke no more, whose hearts weren't quickened by long, moonless night concealing the trees. For the others, spring brought a pale, begrudging sun, the closest thing to God.

Now, as then, people looked on one another without generosity, much as life regarded them. A man worked as his father, deafened in like degrees by the gasoline-powered whine of the circular saw. All day he stood dwarfed among precarious log piles, and he spoke with sawdust lungs to men missing hands and fingers. He lived as his grandfather, as if life flowed always backward. The lumberman's history was never written because all lifetimes held like enough happenings. A person was complete simply knowing what he could see and hear.

Esteem was reserved, not for God or ancestry, self or other, but for a well-known weapon: for the prized Kauhavan blade of the birch-handled hunting knife. If a man went to whiskey when his blade was still sharp, and when he knew the woods, he entrusted the tool to his growing son. The son was new, and the man had known too many winters. The winters finally sunk the man in drink and devoured him; he emerged a little more dreamy each toothless summer, to sit along the riverbanks with his head bent over a bamboo fishing pole.

The son then struck out with fledgling confidence, knowing he would be like the legendary men who skied after elk and let the wind lash their skin and raise it white like blisters. In Poika's mind those men sometimes looked like his father, whose whiskey gave him the strength for work. The two sides of whiskey battled for the man, but nevertheless warmed him within, so that a gleam was hardened in his eyes. In those eyes, sometimes, there was no blue; the eyes were darkened like the forest floor, and Poika saw Indians in them. When he asked his father if the legendary men were Indians too, Karjalainen said: "Anybuddy be anyt'ing."

After Kaukanen went home, Poika lay on his mattress in the attic. His thoughts faltered and dropped off in the night. At times he heard the big man's voice rising up out of the boiling face, and he started. He thought about his father' knife hidden somewhere, about the half-skinned rabbit lying in the frozen mud, and about turning twelve the next summer. He listened to the simple noises in the dark. Then, in thin, exhausted sleep before dawn, Poika felt his own teeth grinding and he heard jeering laughter. The laughter had a dry, parched sound. It was not his own. And then it was not laughter at all, but the late Autumn wind that rushed around the house, whistled over the bulkhead cellar entrance, and fanned the blaze up the unfinished back hall siding. The flames filled the sky, devoured the small house like tinder and finally swarmed into the warm kitchen. Then the crackling was laughter again, laughter filled with all the rage of the crazy Finn himself. Poika woke up and stared. By dawn he had a plan.

THE MORNING WAS BITTER ENOUGH TO snap someone in two, the way frost broke up sunlight on the window. Poika and his father were already scuffling around the house, the boy looking for boots to warm his feet against the wooden floor, and Karjalainen hucking up phlegm into the kitchen sink. Karjalainen knocked over the shaving mug on the shelf and the mirror fell off its nail, upsetting the jar of wide-angled hairpins. He steadied himself against the soapstone basin and shuddered. The pipes churned and the faucet sputtered before a cold stream washed into the sink.

The boy said, "Lookit ya. Ya gut ya long johns on funny. Ya buttons are in the wrong holes. He comes an' lights the house on fire an' you won't be able 'a find the rest a' ya clothes."

Karjalainen tried to focus and center himself in the broken mirror. Then he was coughing and losing his breath and gasping. Poika walked over and with the full force of his weight pounded the man on the back until he was upright again, spreading whipped lather on his hard, brown face. He shaved while the boy walked from door to window, looking for old man Kaukanen. All Poika saw was a local cat approaching the gutted rabbit lying on the ground.

"Go on, get outa there," he said to the cat, but the cat stopped to sniff the carcass before walking on.

"Ol' man Kaukanen jus' betta not come back when we're here," the boy muttered. But his father didn't answer. He only stroked his razor on the strop and snickered, perhaps at some thought of his own. Poika continued talking. We'll hear 'im if he comes. His feet a' so big he can't sneak up on anybody." Karjalainen sank his face into a towel.

"I'm just tellin' ya now," the boy spoke to himself. He stopped thinking about the knife, about school, and even about Kaukanen. He knew about the men of old Finnish songs and stories who were never impressed by fear. He often wondered what had made them strong and what could make him like them.

Karjalainen barely noticed Poika's untied boots moving up to his left. Both headed for the back hall toilet at the same time and Karjalainen flung the swinging door wide open, slamming it into his oncoming son.

"*Saatana . . . ,*" one sleepily annoyed note rang from the boy as he fell back. His father paused before the open doorway to face Poika, just as the opened door sprang back and in turn slammed the man into a backward stagger.

The boy laughed.

A logging arm shot across his chest, cuffed his chin, and pinned him against the wall. Poika's ears reddened. He saw his own cheeks puff; his white-blond hair fluffed itself like a patch of duckling fuzz. His blue eyes opened wide.

"I tellie, *santana perkele* by de neck if 'ee get inna vay," the man shook him. Poika felt the bony frame lumbering over him, the skin brown as a stoat, worn like a shoe all over. The dusky hands pressed sharply into his chest.

Then the man winced as if his breath caught, or he heard something distant. He drew back. Anger was always the same quick lash with him, forgotten before he was finished. He faced the door again and moved dreamily toward it.

"*Saatana, saatana,*" the boy continued in yelps. Then he headed toward the frying pan on the stove, started the fish and potatoes, and brought the plate-covered bowl of curdled butter-milk *bemaa* and *Ravayah*, the Finnish newspaper, from the front porch. Though he was sometimes afraid of his father, little else bothered him when his father was around.

"Ya gut 'ny herring out there, Pa?"

The man appeared from the cold back hall with a tin of brine-soaked fish from the barrel that held the barnacled rock. He set the plate on the table and stood before the boy with a subdued scraping in his breath. His lowered lids lifted showing the steel blades of his eyes. It was the beginning of a nod, the fuzzy churn of voice at the bottom of his throat: friendliness. His knuckly hand reached into the frying pan grabbing the skins off the fresh horned pout that the boy turned with potatoes in salt pork. Poika shook the spatula at the man's ragged, white cotton arms.

"Gimmee ya plate" Poika said, and the man walked to the table to get it, trailed by the clicking tails of his suspenders. While the boy waited, he checked the window for Kaukanen.

Through the window where the cat had been, Poika hoped to see Kaukanen on his way to work. Once past, the man wouldn't be setting flames under their floorboards. At the sawmill, Kaukanen was Hackett's man until well after dark. Then Poika could have all daylight to carry out his plan.

POIKA HAD ONLY SEEN THE MEN in certain situations. He had never seen Kaukanen and Karjalainen on a Saturday toasting beer together with Stepeichik, the Czech, sitting on the river bank among the trees facing the woolen mill on the other side. the men owed their living to the forest. Otherwise they would have worked in the great brick complex and lived in town like the others. From the banking they watched the workers pack bolts of material on the trucks below, and considered themselves lucky. Poika had seen his father's friends out goose hunting. He knew that buildings were too small for them. Walls made Kaukanen dangerous. But Poika never saw them after they'd been hours on the water's edge. Then the three sat in a grunting stupor, having lapsed into their Old Country dialects which made them senseless to one another by the end of day.

IT WAS THE SAME KIND OF MORNING. Karjalainen ate. He ate noisily with his chin stuck out, slurping the heat off the top of his coffee, slamming the cup down. The boy talked. About his school, about his friends, about the things Karjalainen didn't know. His father ate slowly while the boy spoke. Poika put out the bowl of *bemaa* and two heavy glasses, and the man's stretched-out Adam's apple rode up and down his thick gulps. The boy talked loudly over the man's eating and wheezing, but with his brow furrowing every now and then as he looked toward the window.

Karjalainen listened. His pleasure gurgled among his swallows. Then he crammed down the last of his sopping bread. He sat rolling a day's cigarettes and placing them inside the Prince Albert foil tobacco wrapper. He lit one in his mouth and kept it there while he laced his double boots up over the thick woolen socks that held his pants in place. Smothered cursing caught in the coarse fabric of his clothes, and soon he was spitting up the last of his early morning phlegm into the sink, grabbing his plaid wool overshirt and the hat with fur-lined earflaps. He took the Communist newspaper to the stove and threw it into the oven to burn. Then he squinted through the smoke at his son. They were looking in the broken mirror together. The man's face beside Poika's was almost mirthful. He nodded, and then he was off to the sawmill, a flat pint of whiskey fixed in place with his belt.

The slam of the door rattled the window pane. His hobnails tramped across the dirt. Poika watched him go. From his point of view, the man's arms encompassed the woods, and he grew larger as he headed toward the horizon.

This was the time for Poika to return the *bemaa* to the porch, and heave the fish scraps out back. Then he should have followed close behind his father, buttoning up his jacket, setting his wan face against the sun, where the man's dark, hollow face had been. He should have gone over to Hackett's to take up the axe before school, and split red maple for Hackett's winter hearth.

He wasn't doing any of that today. He wasn't going to school with his hand bandaged. He couldn't listen to Oli Tervo, the only other person who earned money trapping at that end of town, or who could match Poika's skill with a twenty-two. That morning Poika had to get rid of the rabbit. Then he needed the rest of the day by the riverbank to carry out his plan. He sat facing the window; his eyes followed the haywire pattern of cracks in the adjacent plaster.

Then he saw Kaukanen outside with his lunchbox, treading the glinting hoarfrost like a dreaming beast; he walked past the clock on the sill, past the napkinholder, and through Aiti's dusty bottle of LaLasine Antiseptic with the faded label. The hardcast frown cut like iron across his face. Fear pounded through Poika. He jumped, and sat up straight. Then Kaukanen was past, gone until nightfall. Poika had ten hours now. The sun moved through the frost on the window and shadows stretched themselves around the dim kitchen, curling in the chairs, filling the cupboard, and deepening the corners.

SOMEWHERE IN THE HOUSE WAS THE hunting knife that had ripped Karjalainen out of his childhood in Finland, and had cut worn lines on ships all the way across. That old steel had nearly cut the throat of the Norwegian farmer who had whipped the fifteen-year-old farmhand every Saturday of that summer. The knife was nowhere in the front room.

Poika searched. The *puuko* was not among Karjalainen's creased pants and good suspenders. It was not with Aiti's purple dress in the bedroom closet. Nothing was hidden there, no pictures or photographs, no curly sisters by a Christmas tree, no old folks standing in snow with fur hats and collars. In Aiti's top drawer he found a few hat pins and tortoise-shell combs, and among shirts and handkerchiefs on his father's shelf a single white button chipped on the edge.

There were no secrets in Poika's home. But he searched. Karjalainen had sold the railroad pocket-watch he won playing poker. Other than the *puuko*, none of their possessions had the power to ward off the night visits of Kaukanen home from the Millstream after work. Even in the lightless reaches of the attic, beyond Poika's mattress in the eaves, there were only tins of salves and boot polishes clutched by frozen cobwebs. In the cellar there were scrub-boards in the set-tubs, and the brown soap that gave his clothes their smell. A barrel contained rags, remains of the worn union suits of all the old man's working years.

Soon the boy was outside buttoning his jacket, facing the hills lined with trees like standing matchsticks. He headed toward the shed which stood in the corner of their acre. The rabbit lay there beside it in the mess of its own innards. Poika heaved it on the frozen garbage in the hardened garden, and he covered the carcass with scraps of hay.

He pulled the shed door open rattling the sprung Yale lock. Inside, the sawhorses were stacked beside bags of cement, upright planks and tins of brads and tacks. Two bamboo fishing poles were hung across a row of nails in the studs; in a can a handful of whiskey bottle corks that the man attached to his fishing lines as bobbers. The fox traps were suspended from the joists, each with Poika's name tag. And his twenty-two was mounted on the wall with the muzzle lowered. Cobwebs cut the height of noon into pale bits of light on the floor.

He did not find the knife. He wanted it, not just because of what he had to do, but because it was the only thing that could soothe his terrible fear. The blade had been worn to half its width by his father and grandfather. It was vested with all the power and luck of tradition. And it was lusterless from lack of use, awaiting revival by the next son. Long gone were his father's nights among strangers in boxcars and hobo jungles. The knife in its last exchange was a stolen thing, taken from the grandfather, an Old World hunter, when he lay sleeping, aspiring to his death in his old man hill of dreams. The thief was his own son, Karjalainen, barely twelve then, who hung on the handrails of a Finnish night train heading south, looking for the lights of civilization.

Poika curled his fingers into the mortise hole in the face of the deep workbench drawer. He pulled with his whole body, then leaned his hip in quickly to stop the drawer from falling on the floor. The files and drill bits inside were rusted and dusty. He saw no steel blade. There was no birch handle, no sheath. He had looked everywhere.

Then he saw a flattened piece of stone, a tooled leaf shape. He recognized the flared form of an arrowhead. The edge was sharp against his fingernail. He wondered if the arrowhead could do the job of the knife. He didn't know where it could have come from. Karjalainen would have shown it to his family if he had found it himself. Maybe the Indian had dropped it that time.

The last time Poika had seen the *puuko* in action was the night the Indian came. Until then the sawmill had been a roving camp, and the people bunked by night around the Glenwood stove. Little territories and towns were finally cleared by the camp all through inland Massachusetts until Hackett set up a permanent operation over at the Gristmill not far from Worcester and bought up property throughout the neighboring towns. The family settled, and Karjalainen built their house in a forty-two night fervor.

One snowy night the angry Indian axed through the kitchen window. He stormed in over the wooden table where Karjalainen ate, spilling the kettle of hot fish chowder on the floor. The boy and his mother were together, Aiti yelling at both men. But his father's body coiled without moving; the stool clattered from under him. The man in skins and long black hair had a crimson face, and he threatened with a raised barking axe. Crazy Canuck Indian from the camp, his mother told Poika later, and something about liquor from the town. The *puuko* flicked in sight from the other side of the table. Two men hissed voiceless words.

Poika saw the metal blade forever after dripping blood and tufts of black hair. His fighting body, sick in the clamp of his mother's arms outside the house heard the blows of fists amidst the screaming of men gone wild. A small charge of neighbors rushed the bloody Indian up the deer trail. Then the people clustered, talking before the house for hours while Karjalainen tore his bread and ate with two teeth missing, and a stony stare, beside the boy doubled over with a stomach-ache at the table, and Aiti's excited cursing that did not stop until dawn.

POIKA LOOKED OUT THE DOORWAY OF the shed. "*Saatana*," he complained, feeling the pain in his hand. He put the arrowhead into his pocket, grabbed the rusty chain of raft shackles hanging by the door, and set out across Varanka's field toward the spruces. The wind tugged the rawhide cords that played at his chin. The field lay like a vast unwalked region. The boy leaned into the cold with his head down. Saws in the distance ripped the November air. He knew that Kaukanen always walked close to the angry river on his way home. Poika headed that way briskly, toward the ice house where the dirt road petered out in the brittle grass.

The south wall of the unpainted structure was propped by a dozen poles; it sagged from years of sun melting the foot-thick blocks inside. The old windows of the huge converted barn were boarded up and the building looked anonymous. The ramp lead down to the lake like a dry tongue awaiting this winter's yield of the lake's hardened blocks. Except for invisible drunks inside insulting each other among the scattered sawdust and hay, the ice house couldn't possibly be known by anyone not living at that end of town, couldn't be a landmark for anyone but the men who felled trees and the boys who chopped wood. The forest reached miles past the rusty dwindling railroad tracks that heaved their overgrowth in an extended mound. The trails started there, and Poika knew the trails without his eyes. He wiped his running nose with his bandaged hand. His heart beat like the sound of quail flushed out of the thicket.

He looked back. The houses were empty. No women warmed them by day. The women were over in the other people's houses, in back kitchens, fixing food and fire. As for the men, the outdoors owned them. They returned to their homes to sleep in sweat and brew. But they always smelled of the outdoors. Its endless reaches showed in their distrustful eyes, and they carried weapons tucked like talismans somewhere in their clothes.

Poika was already one of them crossing the rushing river, with the arrowhead in his pocket, the chain looped around his shoulder. A cunning expression came across his face when he saw the first old tree dominating the surrounding younger ones. It was an oak he had known all his life. In this place, at this moment, he pitted himself against Kaukanen. He knew the strong man's weakness. He set to work quickly with the chain, gashing the bark in several places. The sound was smothered by the river. He stood for a moment, relieved by the sight of the bark's fresh wound. He walked on a little, struck the next tree several times, and felt his excitement rise. In chain marks he plotted Kaukanen's course home.

Poika was light-footed in the forest, and unafraid for the moment. He felt secure in the sound of the river which never slowed even in coldest winter. Then he came to the beech, silver-gray, with dead, pinkish leaves still attached to the branches. The tree had a massive base and a triple trunk. One trunk leaned out over the path and presented a smooth dark bole, like a mask without features, where its lowest branch had been severed. It was a sure point of reference for anyone passing.

Poika took out the arrowhead, stepped up the banking to get his reach, and applied the point very carefully against the smooth knob in the light of waning afternoon. The stone had a very thin edge, and he carved delicately with his good hand. He carved without pressing, going over each stroke again and again. When he was finished, he sat back against an old stump, familiar as an ugly brother. The tree bent toward him, and across the bole where a pair of eyes might be, was blazed the name of 'Marija.' Poika hoped the sight would send Kaukanen back to Gloucester to fish again as he had once in the past, because Marija had been a seaside girl, unhappy in the dark forest. One day her son would have to set her spirit at peace.

Poika whistled a song he had heard on the radio then, and he wandered into the wooded hills. He used the arrowhead to cut brambles for bushwhacking and looked for certain other trees which he stroked with the chain. He climbed the steepest lookout rocks, his private perches in the arms of rotting trunks, squinting out on all below.

From high on the riverbank, the town's twenty-six taverns and nineteen package stores surrounded the mill with the Saturday night steambaths, Kaleva's co-op, and a town hall where movies sometimes came. The row of two-family houses had short back yards that fell off into the river rushing past the mill. He looked on it all: the old pool hall and the Avalon Club in cinders, like the tenements on River Road, where people once gathered in robes and pajamas hurling water from buckets into flames against the night.

Poika was satisfied now that Marija was set to haunt her prey again. He still held the arrowhead feeling with his fingers each place hewn by hand and stone. He wondered if the arrowhead gave him the spirit of the Indians who hunted meat and hides, or if he was now like the old Finns who did the same. Those snow white men ended as gouty invalids sitting on the tree stumps of the North. They finally went stiff one day, their mouths frozen in the gloom of mosses when they had nothing more to say. Giant women came out of the mists and pulled them away on creaking log sledges.

Poika walked as the hunters had walked in the forest, without sound. He moved quietly over dried leaves. The paths he walked were the deer runs of long ago used by the Indians, whose silent history was buried in the forest, and then used by white men when the Indians were gone. Stringy roots caught Poika's toes. He watched the ground too, because the old town drunks came here and died. Boys found them on calm, sunny days, lying under broken trees, their faces bursting purple above rope-cinched necks, with puffed black lips and fingers, and eyes rolled up to the sky.

Poika headed home feeling like a hunter with a bow, and then like a Finnmark Lapp down in the Finnish woods looking for the evasive animals. Aiti said that there came the time when the animals were gone. There were only the hunters, those like Kaukanen who could learn nothing new; and people said those men hunted one another after awhile.

WHEN THE TWILIGHT WAS DIMMING ALL but the outline of trees uphill, and the sawmill was about to quit, Poika began heading home. Sooner than he expected, the darkness rose like a flood on the path below. The sharpness of the cold was gone; the air was calm. His nose filled with spruce and white pine. He smelled the river before hearing it, and sprung from the path down the banking. The river sluiced over a slippery log that he crossed. Seconds later he was on all fours running up the other side, his hand throbbing, reminding him of the rabbit again. Then he stopped short where Varanka's orchard lay with its fallen grasses streaming out of the rising moon. The crabtrees were hunched, all silvered elbows, against the sky.

The dirt road lay there below the hill, and full darkness surrounded Poika's home. There were no sounds, no lighted windows. Nobody was home yet. Karjalainen was somewhere drinking and telling stories. A few lone children might be quietly stoking coals in front rooms, warned to stay home and eat in a pool of lamplight, waiting for their fathers to weave their ways home. Only one sound could be heard, that of a dog barking down on the road. Poika felt the full weight of loneliness.

He followed the dog sound. The spotted animal came around the corner, running up Poika's scent. It was Kaukanen's dog. It nodded abjectly and cowered along in the dirt. Poika rolled the animal playfully with his hands, roughed his fur and tossed him. When he looked up, the ice house loomed. The moon reached down, and again he felt that small dark place of fear deepen in the pit of his stomach. Poika looked around. The dog watched him.

Wind whisked dried leaves across both their feet. The dog listened, its ears were perched above its loosened brow. Then the wind trailed off, and a sound came from within the ice house. Though Poika's blood charged, his heart did not jump. He heard the sound again, a Finnish voice. Poika took a breath. Fortified with the simple power of that afternoon he moved the door open, and entered.

"Where are ya?" He spoke with certainty, anxious to feel his own presence. Shafts of hay spilled from the storehouse loft into the deserted cow troughs below.

"Kaukanen?"

The burly sound repeated: an echo or an answer, the boy didn't know.

"Why ain' ya over Hackett's?" He kept his voice going; he couldn't see in the windowless building. "I thought you were at the Millstream."

When Poika stepped around the ghostly ice cradle, Kaukanen was there, illuminated by a crack of moonlight. He appeared in a thud, as if he had just fallen. He was lying on his back in a pile of sawdust, shining and enormous, drunken and infantlike, with teeth spread across his face like the tines of a hayrake. The dog ran back and forth at Poika's feet, then seated himself with authority beside his master, yet well outside his master's reach.

"What a ya doin' outa work?" Poika wanted to keep his voice up. "I never seen ya outa work so soon."

The man grunted like a beached whale; his crazy white eyes tilted up to Poika, and his hoarse voice scarred by whiskey, mumbled along in a harmless song. The big arm reached out to the boy who jumped back beside the dog. Then the arm flopped in the sawdust and lay gleaming. Poika watched it there. Beyond the man's reach, he was unafraid.

"They gonna be lookin' for ya." Poika kept on, feeling more sure. "They're still workin' over there now."

The man's hairless brow raised and plowed into the rest of his face, roughening his barren features, but the expression slid off his face leaving him with an unfocused frown. He stuttered, nodding as if affirming what he tried to say. The boy recognized the funny appeal of drunken sincerity.

Poika kept talking: "How come ya didn't go to the Millstream?" Kaukanen blubbered in return, words drowning in his own weight. He exposed his gums and rubbed his thighs. At certain angles his face beamed pure moonlight; it became a milky, slippery thing. His lips parted showing his broken teeth. Poika paced before him, probing the real nature of the enemy, white and savage, smelling of alcohol and aged sawdust. In that pool of blubber lolled the full force of menace.

"You never been to the woods today," Poika concluded. Kaukanen's lunchbox was beside him.

Poika talked then as he seldom did. Demons rushed his words. He turned the arrowhead in his hands, and talked about the rabbit, the knife, and the Indians who were gone. He talked beyond being tired, beyond his fear. The words came out in an exhausted flow.

Then he could feel the stillness.

He drew closer to the man. "Akseli?" He used Kaukanen's first name.

The moon had travelled; its light came through another crack in the wall. The man's head was tipped back in harmless shadow. Snores rose out of the deep well of flesh. The noise smothered what the boy was saying, standing in the small off-center shadow of himself. When he stopped speaking, the snores heaved in full fury, as if all sleep had waited to engulf him.

Moonlight crept over the sleeper who had the round face of innocence. Even the dog slept, curled forgetfully in a nest of grass.

Published in *Northwest Review*. Volume XVI-3. Number 3. Summer 1977.

One of 100 Distinguished Short Stories of the Year 1977—in THE BEST AMERICAN SHORT STORIES 1978. Editor Ted Solotaroff speaks in his introduction about painful exclusions of stories (considered when choosing the 20 best)—" . . . there was an arrestingly original narrative by Janet Lindquist Black in the *Northwest Review*—"Poika: 1929"—about a boy struggling with his fear in a primitive Finnish enclave in Massachusetts that again left me leaning eagerly in the direction of its continuation, rather than with the settled feeling of a completed tale."

Suvetar

AITI KARJALAINEN MANAGED THE ENTIRE Hackett household in Concord now, and spent only Thursdays at home. One Thursday afternoon in June, she returned to the middle of town, as she always did, on the blue bus which resembled a toy below the open windows of the mill. Bringing her home seemed the sole function of the bus; she was the last passenger, the reason for traveling so far.

She stepped down onto the bottom step and paused inside the open door. Her fraying hair was pulled away from her face, knotted at the base of her sturdy neck. Firm muscle was couched in the solid flesh of her arms. She felt incessantly capable and alone.

"*Saatana perkele,*" she softly cursed her singing bunions; the sight of the woolen mill provoked her native tongue. Before leaving the bus, she turned back and struck the driver with a frown. An Irishman, he was late, muttering with knuckles white against the wheel while she opened her umbrella outside the door before letting herself into the brash sunlight. Aiti would not face the sun: the light made her daft. Aware of strengths pitted against her own, she thrust the black umbrella overhead and cautiously descended to the curb.

The bus doors clapped firmly behind her, final as the sound of the key turning in the lock of the Hackett's heavy iron gate that morning when she made her way down the long stone pathway to the road. But she did not look back. She was revived by the spirit of beginning again each time she returned to making fishcakes in her own simple kitchen. Sounds of finality happened everywhere, and her eyes sought solace from the hills outside town. There was no need to reopen the past or invite the future to happen too soon. She began a plodding pace along the sidewalk past the wood frame buildings of the town, a summer cotton dress rippling from her shoulders like a breeze-blown curtain.

As she approached the mill, the inland sea gulls were hanging in the air above her crying down, but she did not look up fearing perhaps her winter soul might be obliterated by the daylight. All the while she traveled protected in her own spoked, webbed shadow, mumbling quiet, soothing complaints which relieved her heated heels. She walked firmly as a person touching home ground. She could not know that to the weavers, her return in the blue bus, beneath the open windows of the mill, signaled the middle of the afternoon.

She walked along Main Street as if contemplating an old photograph which revealed nothing new: the worn sepia sameness over time. The community bathhouse was deeply mildewed by vapors rising all winter from the steaming stones. All knew the secrets the steambaths kept of sad, unwelcome births. So many times she had rushed there in still dark mornings to help a poor little one enter the world. She walked into Kaleva's Coop, a clapboard building with cracked and weary paint and second-story window shades in unchanged position week after week, and soon emerged with a full shopping bag topped with peaches, musing all the while about her townspeople, lost like the sea gulls among walls and shadows. Then she brightened thinking that she would soon be sweeping her own back porch set out among the hills.

THE SUDDEN FLUTTER AND CREAK OF the Wayside Diner's screen door startled her and brought her irrevocably home. As she crossed the street, the door flew open and tapped the bright, blank wall, then hung there in the slow groan of the rusted spring. She was instantly captive again in her own circumstances. The stately white houses of the morning sifted instantly from her mind. In the flight of the flimsy door the dark opening revealed a familiar face.

Epi Jernius made her way out of the Diner, muttering and feeling her way like a battered hen, jarring the day with her cankerous complexion and ingrown gaze, her thick, awkward tongue. She stopped and spoke to Aiti with her lipless serpent mouth:

"Jou vass verk for same people too long time," she said, spasmodically jerking her elbow toward the ground. "Look how jou vass valk like dem," her eyes focussed on Aiti's feet as if their throbbing could be seen.

Shaken by her accusation, Aiti was suddenly back in the morning, adjusting and rattling the hands of the Hackett's lethargic clock. But reflecting on that morning's moment, the time was not what was wrong. How long had she been walking Ruby Hackett's walk? The wealthy woman ambled so aimlessly around those vast, uncommunicative rooms. She imagined some great illness of life in that will-less tread: the suggestion of a limp, not outright, but one of missed timing. Now she saw that she had brooded too long on Ruby Hackett, and had unknowingly contracted the burden of someone damaged by resignation.

Suddenly Aiti's old reliable nerve gave way and she saw, like someone dying, the distance from which she had come. Like a fruit whose flesh has been eaten, she had one day arrived at the hard, uncompromising pit of herself. And now the person she had hardened into could suddenly not be found. She started to follow Epi Jernius, but then thought that the figure hobbling away could not have said those words. The woman was merely harmless and ugly, Aiti thought, poor ward of the town, diseased old Finn, as Epi's mother had been: dying of her mother. Through the Diner's side window amid cheap laughter, a broom handle extended Epi's used cup to the rubbish pile. Aiti considered the souffle she had placed on the shimmering surface of Ruby Hackett's table, the chamber music streaming through the parlor door as she polished the majestic bird cage. An involuntary love of everything suddenly seized her. There was nothing but to gather her shopping bag and continue.

THEN WHEN SHE LOOKED DOWN SHE saw the peaches scattered on the ground, each one ripe and glowing against the tarred road. The unbearable peaches were shouting at her to pick them up, and had people not been passing, she would have refused to claim them. But it was too late. She was back again, conquered by the present, the dripping of the alleyways. There were the arms and legs of children kicking out of the open windows. She inhaled the odor of something stale, settled in layers where the light never penetrated. Her recognition was complete.

"I'm coming," she said aloud, as if answering the hills. "Allus I am coming, and soon be home."

At last, the road was empty beyond the river.

Walking there relieved her tired legs because of the soothing shadows of trees. Her body assumed a billowy grace. Her spirit recovered like an evergreen divesting itself of snow, and she moved gently over the countryside as if gathering the whole flock of her separate selves. It was that time of afternoon when the day turns in upon itself with a sustained stillness, as if the sun poured the landscape out of an enormous pause. The umbrella still shielded her from the sun. She was without desire near home, where life held a brief perfection. She surged up McKenna's hill, large and flouncing past the small two-family houses. The thin, abandoned shells of the cicadas rained down from the trees and bounced lightly against the umbrella. The wine of insects dimmed and brightened among the leaves.

She moved along in the octagonal shadow of the umbrella as the center of the panorama spread with the immutable day. Her shadow's changing position was no longer disturbing because of the way distances extended from her like overlapping petals. Her eyes were fixed at the horizon which gave way over and over, continually renewed. But Aiti was not one to rely on renewal. Her steps were never new. They were the same steps over which she advanced and retreated in the course of her existence like the plover at the edge of the waves. Steadily, clearly, setting each foot down, measuring not progression but repetition: the repeated pounding of the earth like waves. Her persistence deepened in the simple fact of her going, guarded from the future by familiarity. But she knew the future happens anywhere, perhaps in something already before the eye. Maybe with whipping wings, the future shows itself to be yet another vehicle, waiting and empty like the small blue bus of an afternoon.

ROUNDING THE CORNER BY ST. BRIDGET'S, she took the shortcut up Cemetery Hill. The chrysalides drizzled past her eyes and rippled on the ground. Rows of houses lay beaming behind her as she entered the field of tombstones where hollow nymph shells were accumulated ankle-deep beneath the trees. She decided to linger in the cemetery, a forgotten garden among wild fields. Losing herself for a few minutes was possible now because her stucco house was so near. The chasing bits of light halted, and the clock began pealing the hour of two. Aiti now almost whimpered. The day seemed about to crack and fall to pieces.

But it was simple to think that now, near home, the day could finally be trusted. The nerves were safe, the bones, the heart. The whole surrounding countryside flowered with impersonal fullness, implying the vast continuation of the present, threaded only mutely with future.

Her future was here in this town where rough, anonymous Finns gathered with whiskey along the riverbanks to toast the passing boats. She smiled thinking of the town fixed like one separate nation against another, the townline as certain of its demarcation as the clock conducting the hour. Nevertheless, uncertainty abounded where the land washed and heaved. Trees fell over borderlines and new ones sprouted. Branches extended their fingers beyond words. The leaves shuddered, laden with the light of Suvetar, that summer spirit which flourishes everywhere like demented appetite.

The place which invited her was a shady place, brown and dusty. She sat upon a broad, sunken monument covered with eager tendrils. Closing the umbrella meant exposing that petrified core of herself which might drift as a dream from beneath the trees. But she was filled with the earned notion of peace. The shopping bag bulged beside her, and over the top of it perched a suddenly brilliant peach. The gift from her employer now felt completely her own. She took the fruit and began eating it there in the music of the cicadas' sublime tin drone. The refrain of two o'clock continued—unanswered—slowing to a perfect moment in the shadows. As if a shout had ended.

In the same perfect moment, a goldfinch alighted on the branch nearly touching her eyebrow, and there was the alarming interruption of a gruff, inhuman voice. From among the tombstones a gaunt, outcast dog with bent and twitching haunches approached her. He had come to claim his mossy sleeping spot behind the stone, and Aiti responded with surprise and a startled pulse.

"I never see you here before," she said to the intruder, and then warned, "in diss place you come to keep quiet." The dog grunted and slouched back to his spot, leaving Aiti disturbed by sudden memory, for her excited heartbeat had marked the real progression of her life.

It first announced itself long ago, like someone inside, and quarreled through her entire youth with virulent craving. The younger sister she had rescued and brought home had been hugged and nearly drowned again in weeping, while Aiti, unnoticed entered the boat that was forever loosened and set drifting. Never to be taken care of, she owed her final freedom to that relentless voice of herself. She had been moved forward by everything she left behind. Her old father was still fixed like a rock to that last fading shore.

In the persistent beat of two o'clock, she saw her overgrown boy running toward her in the distance, his yellow hair erect in the breeze like alerted pinfeathers. His bewildered eyes came into view as she watched him. Her hands were already feeling among the contents of her shopping bag, those hands so definite, yet so anxious when empty. When the boy stopped before her, she gave him the shoelaces. He looked instantly shy and grateful. He stretched them out and studied the long, rawhide chords. They were for his boots. Then he refolded them and dropped them into his pocket. He liked them.

The boy and his mother looked out together, their eyes cast down the rambling and graduated slope studded with gravestones and wild apple trees. They stood still, the woman beneath the umbrella, and the boy facing the sun riding toward the horizon like a gleaming bone. They were struck by the sound of the steeple still reverberating in the sky. But the song was drawn out and distant here. The cemetery pond absorbed the pressing clangor. The thick, dark water quelled the clattering of time and let it ebb defeated to the shore.

They finally spoke of the abundance of Suvetar, that June spirit which belies the coming of winter and the need to prepare. Their voices invited the troubled dog who staggered toward them, sniffed the peach pit lying on the ground, and retired again. They gathered their belongings and emerged from the shadows, and from under the dog's drooping lids, for he held the departing visitors in his dull gaze. With her boy, the woman had a quicker step. The sky was kinder now. The boy had the face of the thrilled young warrior who has not yet seen the slinking beast.

Suvetar is the goddess of the south-wind. Her name comes from the word "suve" for "south" or "summer." She heals her sick followers with honey that she drops from the clouds and protects grazing herds.

Published in *Ararat—A Quarterly*. Special Fiction Issue. Issue No 82. Spring 1980.

Loyal Opposites

BECAUSE OF HER CLARITY, GAINED by never sleeping, Amanda was really the first to understand that her father was taking over the whole house, transfiguring it with new forms and materials.

He began slowly with one quiet living room window, low and free form, molded in polycarbonate, without corners or right angles, like a floating, out-of-focus bubble rising up the white plaster wall. Set almost precisely at an eleven-year-old's eye level, it looked up the banking of ferns that faced that side of the house and it was tipped slightly out at the bottom to capture the cool, accurate northern light.

Claire had remarked that their friend Eileen's Great Dane was almost able to lift his leg on his view of the living room, but her husband's deep mood cleared for a moment and he looked hurt. Then a similar window was placed high up on the kitchen wall almost near the ceiling. From a suspended crossbeam, Hunter hung by his rock climbing fingertips for long minutes contemplating the sky outside, his eyes full of a resinous languor. Amanda saw that her mother was actually unable to eat lately, she seemed so disturbed by the window and by Hunter's new intention to treat their house as an object.

Amanda knew that all of her father's schemes progressed to outrageous obsessions, that the ends had been mildly, if unconsciously conceived in the beginning, and that ultimately he quieted down. But this time Claire's reaction seemed overwrought, unlike herself. She gagged several times while eating a peach one morning. Because it was their house. They had finally declared it completed a year ago—entirely done: by themselves. Yet Hunter seemed determined to overhaul their combined, finished effort, as if to assert his "self" over synthesis. He engaged his friend Claude as architect and moved with the fire of all his hyper creative schemes. But if caught unaware lately, Hunter could be seen looking mournful and weary, sometimes almost febrile. As if somehow opposing whatever enigma had overtaken his spirit, he began to show the driving, exclusive ambition of someone forging a personal rite.

Erin, the first-born twin daughter, placed one of Hunter's own hand-tooled pewter crescents in the window and set a tall beeswax candle into the copper valve embedded in the material. The window had a molded sill of clouded polyurethane that almost resembled ivory, in the shape of a spent wave ready to be drawn back by the tide.

Amanda, her identical sister, was disturbed by the window, saw it more as a break than a change. The window caused her a shock of troubled caution, the way she felt when the mead wine was allowed beyond the mellow stage because Hunter failed to loosen the caps to release the carbon dioxide gas. The carefully fermented wines stood shelved to the ceiling of Claude and Eileen's cold cellar next-door and then forgotten long past peak flavor. Amanda felt dangerous about it, but Erin followed her father's shifts of energy better. Much of the wine was passable. Hunter had designed the whole operation but was naturally bored by details of maintenance. He was thrilled by Erin's candle, and he seemed soothed, even though Amanda didn't smile, when she said she kept watching the window for schools of fish.

Hunter played with physical properties, Claire thought, as a balance to the abstract, molecular level of his work. He had never touched the field of anatomy which his father had dominated for decades, except to take his MD. Hunter was tall, and in the unexotic environment of an elite, small undergraduate college he had worn an orange, hooded Moroccan cape which to this day hung limp and fuzzed with aging on the back of the kitchen door, a misfit-looking thing inside of which he appeared to be flying. He only wore it outside the house occasionally. But it had been his pet mantle in that indulgent, flamboyant, studious life on which both he and Claire had so thrived together at the beginning of a vital era when Dylan danced beneath the diamond sky.

Claire had been talking now about returning to mass spectroscopy. Her family had a black side and a white side, both equally acquainted with chauffeurs and riding breeches in New Orleans, both about the same shade of flesh, only their stages of arrival were of different vintage. Together Claire and Hunter had traveled throughout the Far East for eight months before earning their advanced degrees and finally settling on the north shore of Massachusetts.

The round, brass Persian tray with fluted edges was set on its graceful driftwood base, the wood sanded and polished by Hunter, who had found it on the shore near Plum Island. That table was placed slightly to the right of the window. Set out on the tray was the burnished copper samovar they had bought in Turkey; its shadow lengthened over the gray blue Bokhara in the course of the afternoon.

Beyond that, from the ceiling, hung the wicker basket-seat lined with batiked cushions. Next to it was Hunter's latest invention, a seven-foot length of five-inch flexible plastic drainage pipe, elbowed and serpentine, one end conveying light from a bulb in the wall, the splayed other end emitting its flow for the reader seated in the cushioned basket. No one quarreled with the very particular arrangement of that wall. But Amanda was bothered to the degree that the design was her father's vision alone.

The Nakamura bench filled the space to the left of the window. A raw, planed, six-foot-long plank of South American mahogany was fitted with an upright cherry dowel backing which resembled the strings of a lyre. The legs were smoothly turned, and the seat had the flowing edge of unfinished lumber that rhymed now with the windowsill. Claire and Hunter had conceived of the bench together, as they had the cedar-lined shower stall and the redwood bathtub. Up to this stage, everything in the house had been an effort of joint consideration and enthusiasm. Amanda could feel the alienation her mother suffered because of the window by which Hunter separated himself. Claire had recently grown so much thinner. Amanda watched her from the bench. The couple had worked together with Nakamura to design the piece which was comfortable even to lie on. It was true; with a cushion for the head, the cool silky wood was as soothing as a piece of chamber music.

Hunter said at dinner that the time had come to remodel. Amanda almost turned her glass of slightly oxidized Muscat onto the carved eucalyptus coffee table where their meal was spread overlooking the blue Bokhara, and she shifted her cushion back from the table. Their mother had made Billi Bi and presided over the cauldron with the ladle, but her commanding roundness was not there. Behind Claire, four colorful flat-weave Peruvian rugs were mounted on the wall above the bench, one with an orange frog that haloed Claire's head in a crimson scream: ecstatic or horrified, loud or silent.

Claire's relatively sudden weight loss had changed her. She looked at Hunter, but her former implicit power was missing without the quantity of her face. Her cheeks had lengthened, and with her hair drawn back by a scarf, she appeared almost childishly large-eyed, without the tidal serenity of her fullness. Her whole form had changed and made a different statement. the amber drop-earrings emphasized contours beneath the cheek-bones that were never there before. Amanda was frightened by her mother's sudden silence, saw in those eyes a kind of blighted emotion that made her features resemble a still-life arrangement. Amanda noticed too that her father's beard had grown, a sign of his wilder, crazier self emerging his "*wereself*" she called it, in which a new vacant or regardless expression appeared full of some riddle of inspiration, some veiled wonder visiting.

No sooner had Claire spoken to Hunter recently about his postgrads—the most talented and admiring of whom felt he had somehow suddenly tightened their reins—than he suffered an attack of sciatica. He had not been happy confined to bed for three weeks around his thirty-eighth birthday with pain burning and shooting down the backs of his thighs and in a valium stupor. As some untouchable privacy grew within him, so his beard became manifest, and so the house began undergoing its change. Amanda watched him sleeping once and felt deceived by that peaceful-seeming submissiveness. The trust she felt was terrible because it was not true. Her father seemed lately to have a more obscure source, a deeper puzzle as to where he began, and in his waking moments he did seem to be changing as rapidly as a mountain stream, renewed and forging a wider, faster course, drying up in its original places.

Amanda had drawn a portrait of her parents when she was six. The picture was framed and hung in the kitchen. They looked like two Apaches, each with long flying hair, wearing similar suede jackets with fringed sleeves, and bonded by a clasp of hands. It seemed impossible that they were no longer young now, as if something were shoving them out of being themselves. Both had gray wires among their rich, black hair, and some of their spunk and sureness had been humbled. Claire's whistling around the house had taken on a more involuntary and unconscious, less wishful, tone than before. But it didn't seem possible that they could really lose touch with the vital thing they were.

After dinner, Erin was lying comfortably back on her cushion listening to the crystal softness of the beginning of Beethoven's Ninth with the wrapt look of someone wearing earphones. She stared through the immense glass wall which faced the forest. The room was acoustically perfect now, and they had given their earphones to Claude and Eileen. But Erin had the look of someone plugged in, hearing nothing else, and the flame in the window exhibited perfectly the motionless intensity of that beginning theme, and at the crescendo the fire imperceptibly wavered and the shadows of the room pulsed. Only the music, but none of their voice frequencies affected the flame. Amanda was not in harmony with the room, not with her drawn-looking mother, her newly bearded father, or her untroubled sister. She didn't want to go to bed or to sleep. Amanda never slept, but absorbed and monitored every sound of the night, especially her sister's breathing, while Erin sprawled, willingly drowning in headlong sleep, serene as the lengthening shadows that poured themselves away from the morning light. One night recently, Amanda had gone down to the kitchen just before midnight for a glass of milk. With her eyes on the blithe, almost stick-figure portrait of her parents, she overheard her father tell Claire that he and she had done more than begin to look alike; he said in a pathetic voice that he was afraid they had somehow become inbred.

AMANDA BEGAN CLEARING THE BILLI BI off the table. She left the room to wash the dishes, to be alone. It was late, but she dreaded going to bed. Claire had said it was impossible not to sleep, but Amanda finally realized she was trying to tell her mother that she didn't dream. All night she knew the pattern of one moth in the room, the changing shadows, as if no cushion of inner life existed between herself and reality. She didn't even know what it was like to dream. When she last persuaded Erin to reveal her dreams, Amanda cried while listening.

EVEN WHEN THE WINDOW OPENINGS BEGAN filling every wall of the house like floating holes of light, even when the scraping and mixing of polyurethane foam began with Claude and his partner, Vachot, in the early morning and when increasing arguments echoed up from downstairs, Erin's depth of unconsciousness was not touched. Her sleep was a fixed thing. Amanda was hurt by it. Erin's arms and legs were strewn, as forgotten as the laundry their great, great grandmother dumped down the stairs when word arrived that slavery was ended. Erin slept, her limbs cloaked in smooth, amnestic lilac.

Amanda didn't forget anything. All night, she was aware of the room around her, of what Erin was doing, of what everyone said. The girls bore their parents' travesty in separate ways. Erin slumbered through the arguments as if the two sides of battle upheld each other, formed a well-made bridge. She was more apt to be disturbed by unevenness, by the withdrawal of one or the other, but this rarely happened. Either both shouted or both were silent, and Erin was secure in the predictable symmetry of their dialogue. She liked her mother's thinning, rejuvenated look reflected by Hunter's lengthening beard and hair. The house was changing fast, losing its corners and straight lines; tortuous passages within narrowed and meandered, then widened into cozy dens. From outside it looked as if Hunter had conceived of mushrooms—four enormous growths in the forest filled with skylights newly lighting the inside of the house in the design of a sundial so that the fall of light perfectly demonstrated the hour.

His extremes were forcing his wife out, and Amanda feared that her mother was taking the path of disappearance.

If dreaming was part of life, then sleeping became worse than movies. Amanda talked and nudged her sister all through movies on Saturday afternoons to relieve the panicked loneliness she felt at Erin becoming so exclusively engrossed, especially through repeated sittings at an old version of "Last of Mohicans" shown at the Fine Arts, the same version their father had seen seven times as a boy.

Amanda was caught in an idea she could not escape. She dreaded the day when she and her sister looked at one another the way her parents did, blank and helpless, each wishing the other could act. It seemed, watching her parents, that anyone could find herself someday lost in an increasingly private maze beyond anyone else's touch or communication. It terrified her to think that she or Erin could experience an event the other might never know. They must try very hard to duplicate their experience or frightfully lose touch. Not in the important things. The remarkable events would always be shared and re-counted, but the slight, barely perceptible happenings of daily life would slip through the sieve of time, to be forgotten and amount to their unfathomable separateness, the aloneness of anyone.

ONCE A BRIGHT SPOT, THE ORANGE cape seemed to be actively fading now, pounced over its peg on the kitchen door. No longer did Hunter throw it over his shoulders and rush like a bizarre Zorro into the cool night to add garbage to the compost. Nor did he wear it on summer evenings, which they used to spend outside, almost always with friends, when music flowed from speakers set up in the trees—when every adult was intoxicated in at least three ways, and Amanda thought of her father in spirit as Country Joe McDonald who had the American flag glistening on his right front tooth. That was when Hunter used to sing and surround Claire with his orange cloak in the cool darkness.

He had made Claire some surprising gifts of affection in the past. He had bronzed her gardening shoes: her ultimately laceless high school sneakers full of frayed holes which corresponded to callouses on her little toes. They were always set on the mat inside the back door, squat and bulging with the tirelessly adhesive sucking mud of spring, as if all her mudded tracks had come along with the feet that made them.

"Gardening in the rice paddy," Hunter had commented, looking at those shoes which resembled two pieces of amateur pottery waiting to be fired. Then one day he presented them to her—bronzed, mud and all—as a pair of bookends, together with a new pair of sneakers. That was when Hunter and Claire regarded themselves as special together.

AMANDA SPOKE ABOUT SPECIALNESS. BUT Erin missed the point that being twin-born was a special opportunity, and often reacted as if Amanda was bizarre when she pointed out one broken streetlight in a row, a squirrel on a branch, a tan Chevrolet.

"A tan Chevrolet! So what, a tan Chevrolet?"

"I was afraid you might not notice it too."

"You sure are getting spooky."

"But Erin, I wouldn't even notice these things, if I didn't have to tell you about them. You make me more aware."

Claire was concerned with awareness of many kinds, on many levels. A person could pass through life not really knowing what he himself was doing and thinking. Or one could pains-takingly develop an alert consciousness, fed by every little thing all over the landscape. Claire's own cultivated alertness never flagged. She spotted everything. Thought went into her actions. Claire always knew just where she was, she seemed to hold the thread of the entire route into or out of any present condition. It wouldn't seem that she could get into trouble.

After Claire and Amanda met with Amanda's teacher, the three stood talking in the school's new gymnasium. It had surprised Miss Kingsley that Amanda so pleasantly agreed to meeting with a certain Dr. Strout. But now they discussed the poetry course arranged for next year, while Amanda's eyes followed one warm, school-bus yellow stripe which two young men were applying around the edge of the basketball court. Something about the stripe tickled her inexplicably, it had a melting, almost friendly, comic spirit, the way it went humming around the floor. Then she saw that Claire was focused on that same animating stripe too.

In her mere eleven years, Amanda had come to trust those experiences most which edged on unconscious obscurity. Those perceptions that were barely events slid into the mind unnoticed and lodged in obscure crevices; never reckoned with, they governed moods and actions with more subtle control than even associations of color, rain, fog, or sun. It seemed that holding these unremarkable things, telling them, sharing them, kept people whole and mutually recognizable, preventing willy-nilly private notions from grabbing one's elements and breaking and charging away, the way her parents and friends failed to sustain faith and wholeness. Amanda would defy anything short of death itself that lessened her hold on those same people who closely surrounded her own beginnings. She refused the mortality inherent in relationships.

Because of the yellow stripe and similar trivia, Amanda could feel how much her mother was with her, just because she was *there*, because she absorbed their entire surroundings. Driving home, Claire began with one droll comment that the orange-haired, green-eyed Miss Kingsley looked like Van Gogh's sister. Amanda was amazed as they talked by the details her mother had noticed, from Miss Kingsley's veery voice to the smells of materials being used to build the new gym. She had even noticed that the plasterboard walls throughout the school were green.

"Erin," Amanda cried. "This tan Chevrolet is a moment that will never happen again."

"But do you really think it makes any difference?"

"Yes," Amanda replied painfully. "Our whole life."

ERIN ENDURED AMANDA'S PREDATORY attentiveness but without much conviction or encouragement. She didn't say that Amanda didn't *have* to tell her anything. She felt guilty for being the well-adjusted one. She had tired first of fooling everyone by exchanging places in classrooms, while Amanda felt obligated to the trick no matter how silly. The girls' resemblance was exactly mirror-image. Any new person mistook one for the other until knowing them well. It was not as if one's face were rounder, or one were noticeably taller or heavier. Erin was a quarter inch taller and right handed. Both had their mother's eyes, slightly Asian and neat—"like eyes of a canary," Erin once said; "or the pretty green snake," Amanda added.

While Claude was working on Hunter's house, he and Eileen separated. Eileen was Claire's best friend, and remained next door while Claude moved out. The girls learned the story from Henry, their older boy. First Claude's younger brother, also an architect, had died of a heart attack at age thirty-six, fell behind his power mower which kept going around the lawn like something crazy running away. Then Claude had turned forty and informed his wife that they had both cast themselves in too narrow an existence. He immediately quit smoking, turned to a salt-free diet, and vacated his home.

"Well," Amanda had suddenly informed Henry, "our father is building our mother out of our house," Erin had flinched with surprise. "We'll all be gone when it's finished, and he'll be alone." Amanda added: "He's declared war."

Henry moved out with his father. After that he saw the girls so little that he began mistaking Erin and Amanda for one another.

There were times when Amanda imagined that only one of them would be the concert violinist both sisters wanted to become. Both already had the middle fingerprints of one hand worn smooth. They would practice hard as children, not knowing the outcome, exactly like their mother who had perfected her ballet and then grew too tall to be a professional dancer.

Amanda understood that their challenge was really her own; she had to dramatize and embellish her observations to gain Erin's interest and to disguise her apparent trivial level of concern.

"Does that woman remind you of Grandma?" she asked Erin on their way to Rudi's restaurant for Saturday lunch, as a way of getting her simply also to notice the person seated on the park bench. "She has dangling, Spanish-looking earrings like Grandma, and a gorgeous hand-knit sweater . . .

The woman did resemble Claire's mother, whom Claire described—with her long midnight-and-silver braids—as an aging Princess Summer-Fall-Winter-Spring. But Amanda had used the ploy before, and Erin was not interested.

"I can't picture her belly dancing," she persisted and laughed because they both enjoyed their grandmother's eccentricities.

"I think that woman is a quadroon," Amanda said, and then Erin turned reflexively.

"My God, Amanda, you concentrate so hard," Erin finally remarked.

THE DORMER WINDOWS WERE replaced by polycarbonate shapes similar to the one in the living room, each one individual, free form, like dreams. They were fixed in place by the cast plaster-foam outside, the color and shape of shelf moss which took three days to set fully. From outside the effect was one of a crop of wasps' nests or poured cast globs of pudding.

"Bosoms," Claire said, "massive buff-colored breasts."

Claire's tolerance now had an alarming, flat permissiveness, a self-abdicating side that suggested she was untouched by the walls reshaping all around her, or that she was biding her time, saving up for something. She ate almost nothing now. The girls' room with new windows north and east took on the sense of innerness, the outside peering in, pressing shadows of vegetation against the floor. The windows seemed to pressure one inside. The light and the liquid shapes seemed indefinite, recreating the tops of trees on the floor. The leaf forms spread and marched in diurnal sequence by sunlight or moonlight and made one feel at the bottom of a pond. The interior became increasingly convoluted and it grew more difficult to find one another inside.

One high skylight cast a fall of sun to the bottom of the stairwell, and Hunter lay plastered motionless to a foam rubber mattress that was covered with an African print, his ponderous overflow of hair, his pitch-dark eyes full of other business. Both his daughters thought the spot was lovely and peaceful, and even Amanda snuggled there with her father a few times. Claire joined him now and then in the twilight to drink sake and reminisce about old times. Once Amanda saw them searching one another for mosquito bites, as if they had forgotten the recent past, but, in the act of growing older, they seemed to have irreparably betrayed each other.

One day when Claude's partner, Vachot, stopped working at noon to take a break, Claire sat with him on a flat slab of rock in the middle of the drying stream bed, below the house. She wore her long skirt and sandals with a sleeveless cotton knit; her long hair spread like seaweed as it always did when she didn't tie it back. The hair which used to flow out from the generosity of her face now drew out the uneven hollows. Claire told Vachot that day what Hunter had said about their inbred look.

"Do you feel trapped too?" Vachot had asked.

Claire answered: "Only in that my husband is becoming a tragic stranger . . . building himself a maze to hide inside." They talked further while Amanda hopped the rocks in the stream.

"That he is doing this, somehow in reaction to me," Claire continued, "makes me an accomplice. I am helping to create the monster."

Amanda left them sitting. It was suddenly not so clear to what extent she was Claire's replica, to what degree Erin was so comfortably, unchangeably Hunter.

SMOOTHLY, ERIN SLEPT, SECURE AND swaddled in pliant purple folds. Amanda's own pale yellow comforter looked like a mess of scrambled eggs at the foot of the bed. Her pillows were on the floor, the soft one on end in a blob. No longer did Amanda prowl the house during the night as she did when small, crawling into her sister's and parents' beds, pressing her ear softly to each one's chest to listen.

"Amanda, you can't keep waking me up all night asking me to tell you my dreams."

Dr. Strout had asked Amanda what it was like to be a twin, and she had replied after some thought: "What is it like not to be?"

"I only wake you, Erin, when I see rapid eye movement," she explained. "I'm afraid you'll forget your dreams, or die of fright if you have a nightmare."

"You can't watch me sleeping all night. It's creepy. An invasion of privacy. Sleep is personal, important, necessary for survival . . . Go to sleep, Amanda!"

"Erin, I'm like a light that stays on. I think I'd die if I slept."

"Amanda, you have to get over this."

Amanda pictured Erin's sleep like the forest the poor babes got lost in, boggy and webby and strangely long ago, allowing no sound, with giant shafts of light warming ripe blackberries on the vine, fermenting the juice, stirring a swarming day-shift of silent bees to work. Erin sat at the foot of a tree so gigantic she resembled a tiny mushroom, one of the boletus from the backyard that Claire found described in the field guide. Of course, Amanda pictured herself there too, a twin boletus, "identical to the teeth," as another doctor had once said, displaying the dental x-rays that had completed their twin study charts. She did not know why the forest of Erin's sleep must be silent. Maybe because in the song the children never got out.

The sisters had not split up yet. But the effort to hold together was Amanda's alone. Only she recognized the opportunity as one most people don't have. Erin seemed generally tolerant of the endless energy of her sister's observations. But she had no idea of the depth of her sister's scheme. Amanda couldn't stop herself; she was constantly fixing details in Erin's mind, and in turn ferreting out Erin's thoughts and ideas, watching Erin's eyes, where they settled; out a bus window, or on the pattern of a spoon. It was much more than a game to Amanda. It actually hurt her that they could sit facing one another in Rudi's restaurant watching different people, overhearing separate conversations, registering opposite halves of the room, becoming divided by finitude. She always waited for Erin to order first, then she ordered exactly the same. It didn't matter that Erin yelled at her. She didn't want to lose her sister.

Hunter painted and carpeted the interior of the house while Claire and the girls conveniently visited her mother in New Orleans for a few days. Amanda had an experience there which she wanted to tell her mother about some day. Their grandmother had rearranged her house a bit, and the girls, each having taken a healthy helping of Indian pudding the first evening, were walking to the living room to eat seated in the huge, comfortable living room chairs.

"Look how fast the ice cream is melting, Erin," Amanda began to say, facing her sister and thrusting up the bowl with a vanilla pool spreading and running over the steaming cornmeal-and-molasses pudding. The hallway was dimly lit. But her sister shocked her. If looked as if Erin's lips moved in exact unison with her own, strangely mocking; and with a dizzying unreality, Erin's bowl too moved forward exactly as Amanda's, with the same gesture in time. Too late, Amanda faced not Erin, but herself—in the old mirror with the burled wood frame—moved from their grandmother's bedroom and reinstalled downstairs. Amanda remained fixed in the mirror for some time, knowing something she was seeing would not come away with her. A strange, permanent longing began in that spectacle of her sister turning into herself.

HUNTER'S ENTRANCEWAY WAS MOLDED narrowly, and plush-paneled in shades of red from top to bottom. The ceiling had recessed lighting.

"Like a gullet," Claire commented with no expression. "I feel as if I'm walking into someone's tonsils." Without setting down her suitcase, she toured the shapely, red, widening and narrowing interior that had been her home.

"It is really a womb inside," she explained to Eileen after leaving, her suitcase still in hand. "A bosomed creation with a labyrinthine uterus inside."

Later that night, a glimpse of Hunter's garrison from Eileen's kitchen window startled Amanda. There in the glowing darkness was her father's silent door. There was his house in all its suffering and limitation. Here were her mother and sister slack-shouldered with an emotion that was all too inexact. There had been no stroke of providence, only their family idly fretting into petulant destruction.

She walked back to her father's house in the still dark morning like the last straggling daughter of a broken tribe. She threaded her way along one passage into the center of the tragedy her father had built. He was seated looking aged and desolate, wracked like herself by a sleepless night. Undulating shapes surrounded him as if he were afloat beyond the shore, the stream having emptied itself finally into the sea.

But all she could do was question how he could cause them to go away like that, without sorrow or anguish, only disturbed and displaced.

"I felt worse for Uncas and the Mohicans," she said, finally.

Hunter tried to say something.

Then they were both surprised when the day's first sunlight leaped like a sudden messenger through the dawn window.

———————

Published in *The Kenyon Review*. Volume IV. Number 4. Fall 1982.

The Gift

DIANA'S GIFT TO JUSTINE FOR HER thirtieth birthday was a potted fuchsia chosen by some study of astrological charts which Justine did not understand or believe, and grown by Diana herself, who had a superb green thumb. From a cutting started exactly on Justine's previous birthday, this spatially balanced hothouse form of life had secretly undergone a whole gestation with her in mind, and now emerged in an aerial, circular patterning of drooping floral heads, to sit on Justine's polished round oak table: a showy evening primrose, with corolla on the uncanny mauve spectrum of her mother's perpetually 'dying-starlet' slippers, and a cadillac kind of obviousness which surprised Justine, given the more contemplative plane of her personal taste.

Glad for the obliterating darkness, she opened up the sofa bed and stretched out before the empty fireplace with the dog, as she did every night now that she slept alone.

Foliage of trellised morning glory peered in at the windows. A faithful streetlight out by the rutted dirt road silhouetted the twining stem and leaf shadows all over the plain bed sheets. She drew up the calico coverlet on which she had exactly copied this shadowed design in a rambling pattern of zig zag strips in black and ivory freehand appliqué with swags of terra cotta and luminous blue invisibly hemmed to the background; then her hand-sewn darning stitch coursed in energetic arabesque tendrils over the ten-foot square.

But in the breaking dawn, the potted fuchsia dominated the whole first floor with its shrill, glowing concentration of color. Justine felt vaguely hostage; those aggressive fluted bells and their perverted stinger hovered more blatant than anything else in the room. Something about herself that was never touched seemed vaguely interrupted. The inner weight-bearing walls of the old farmhouse had been replaced by post and beam, giving a vast, warm and open stretch of living space, but without a place to hide, and the riveting intensity of those blossoms grabbed the eye from every corner.

Certainly she and Diana had a healthy difference of point of view. And this was a thoughtful gift. The fact that they were neighbors, and both artists, fixed them in the permanent relationship of members of a tribe.

Her own miniature gouaches on the wall depicting her student life became lost like little birds photographed without the telextender. There were the dark, gliding swans of that last memorable spring at Cambridge, so minutely correct on a supple brim of aqueous color, and the four friends she had drawn from a photograph and imposed along "mathematical bridge" in medieval Cloister Court. The picture included herself with her open expression as earnest as a young boy's.

These early efforts were far behind now, but she always admired with grateful satisfaction the precision of detail and adroit rhythm of her line, whenever she sat facing them to speak on the telephone. Then, leading toward the window from those pictures were her oils of root patterns in a stunning leaded sienna bronze pigment scumbled on paper: all upright, feathered, frayed and tenacious within the earth, some of them softly gnarled in the gentle persistence of gripping. All these had composed a formation of unity: the friends so perfectly captured on the bridge, a procession of chimneys on Trinity Lane, the two dusky, moving swans, the root patterns and then, three burly pine knots, vaguely winged, rising up the recessed window frame: some former self in migration toward the freedom outside, heralded by the blue, trumpeting morning glories.

Of course, her large, luxuriant "Chance"—an appealing zygote-like organism in bright acrylics merging into a half-tone field, with surfaces both transparent and opaque, built up to suggest depth—was primordial in sense, and bore the artist's given stamp of colors: the deep, lustrous mahogany and harvest-yellow of her eyes and hair. It had been called the firmest triumph of her first gallery show. The creature on the table upstaged this whole north wall. Even before she began reasoning with herself anew this morning, Sky awakened barking the way he had retired, his nostrils moist with uncritical spontaneity over a new thing.

Later she went outside to bury fish heads among the tomato plants. Then, returning through the front door with an armful of zucchini and cabbage, she was further surprised, because the eye spotted the flowers instantly, before the mind. Their jarring reflection appeared in the window like an explosion of fireworks. She never liked easy beauty. Her resistance was reflexive. But this gift horse harbored within itself an intent little army out to conquer her will. She forgot about it for a moment. Then, there it was behind her in the bathroom mirror; sudden, yet sneaking persistent.

Beethoven could not drown out its high frequency. The Ninth vested it with a stilled, holy intensity, then an oppressive soprano gale. The fated velvet voice of Jim Morrison heated the whole living plant to a sensual vulnerability, and California Latin Jazz made the blossoms quicken and throb like pinched earlobes pressed from within by dammed up blood. Music only added to the plant's command and to the pitch of the dog's bark, so that Justine finally coaxed Sky out of the back door to be rid of him for the afternoon.

Sky was an enormous, rust-colored mongrel with thick, flagrant hair which gave him the shape of a spreading brush fire. Justine had made one of the great mistakes of her life in failing to discipline this vigorous creature because, more than with herself, she had tried to allow pure freedom to a living thing, to let it wander out of bounds. When she walked, sometimes for unaccountable hours, around the reservoir, or up Brodie Mountain, he charged in straight courses up and down the slopes, exciting bursts of quail, or causing a doe to leap in arcs screaming to camouflage its young. In his direct, instinctive character, Justine thought Sky perfectly embodied the traditional idea of expressionism. Sky's energy was that of something in revolt, though ingenuous, his protest unwitting.

But Sky's freedom for Justine, was continually punishing. He wandered; and she was forced to drive from farm to farm along the mountain road apologizing if he'd dug up flower beds, snatched an undershirt from a clothesline, or cornered a chicken. Once, he chomped right into the front of her sister's weekend house and left a rough, ragged tear in the siding so that he was banned from further visits. After he did something wrong, his eyes grew sad and sensitive, and Justine knew all the difficulty he experienced in living with himself—because he was uncomplicated, and thrived on simple attention and praise.

But, new tricks—of course—became impossible by the time she realized her own errors. Around the house, the dog chewed up her sketchpads every now and then, or swished one of her hand-thrown, carved raku pots to the floor with his tail. Once, during their inauspicious start together, he fought her for a hamburger, their only showdown ever, in which she was forced to succeed in establishing necessary command. When he showed up with a dead, limp duck, she plucked and hung it for a day. The last time she invited Diana for Peking duck, Diana spent some fussy effort in blending a special salad dressing. The ducks seemed lately to have learned to stay away.

Without Sky, Justine was alone in the house. This plant was a perfect gift, timely and penetrating. Diana had chosen the right moment of weakness, knowing how Justine suffered over her seemingly failed marriage, over her whole changing point of view and purpose which faltered and redirected itself endlessly since moving to the country. She sold all the first descriptive landscapes she had done from her sister's locale, before she lived nearby herself: scenery depicted in sharp focus which had accomplished the crystalline light of exact moments. These had all been sketched and painted from various heights and projections and angles of that particular setting, broken up into frames of time and vision, into the shadings of certain weekend visits and momentary awarenesses. Following this aroused passion for nature, Justine had then moved here to be within its actuality. Then, almost immediately, she ceased the literal treatment of the subject she now lived, turned her paintings over to be sold, and realized in retrospect a profitable metier. These landscape creations then progressed into varying degrees of abstraction which expressed an increasingly mysterious depth of personal artistry. Later her outlines became more discreet and textures more flat.

Beauty seemed everywhere around her in the country. Her chance emotional life assumed the surprise and pleasure and continuity that she had expected from successful composition. Moved by a new rhythmic steadiness that was personal, she turned to the applied arts for a time, became interested in textures of fabric, clay, wood: textures adapting the abstract designs of her last paintings until visual sensation became satisfyingly resonant on the flat, two-dimensional surface. The quilts seemed a more living form than the paintings. Quilting, pottery, weaving and even her clumsy carpentry were all applicable to living, utilitarian, if one thought of life as a kind of surrounding room. These lent beauty to dailiness and gave another dimension to the exhilaration she once felt exclusively toward objects of display which seemed forever above life, much like the exotic, potted plant.

Now, again, her attitudes were different. Two days of every week were devoted to designing quilts by commission, working together with an apprentice who carried out the execution. The rest of her time was spent painting in her barn-studio, concentrating on three-dimensional movement with the renewed force of a spring charged mountain stream.

As the afternoon wore on, the gift from Diana became so puzzling, that Justine was forced to wonder about her friend. If it didn't express Justine, it didn't express Diana either. The blossoms seemed so cherubic and whining, as styled as something done in the eighteenth century. Both women were courageous in different ways: Diana on a direct course in her work which grew ever more technically analytic and perfectly balanced, highly based on perspective. While Diana loved company, she was never troubled during times when she lived alone. Both preferred the rural setting, away from the plundering anonymity of cities. But Diana always reached for experience beyond the ordinary realm at hand, while Justine's artistic sensibility derived exactly from the commonplace, and, like the early Flemish masters she loved, she felt all the conviction of the infinite within her immediate scope.

Justine lived on the edge of the forest, her home bounded by a ruffling field. With constant care, she kept the two separate, for saplings marched daily like barbarians into the field to lay claim, and Justine regularly cut some of them back. She was somehow clear about the distance to be maintained between home and forest. By placing small mounds of compost all over the back yard, she led a tangled carnival of absurd hybrid squashes practically to the door. These happy vines suppressed the growth of trees, and the enormous leaves of zucchini resembled seats one could ride in a great flying manège. Diana was generally less solitary than Justine, in certain moods more drawn to city dazzle. At those times Diana enjoyed displays of personality, and sometimes styled herself with edible looking makeup. Justine teased her about her enviable public manner, her smooth charm and lack of scruple about embracing everyone as her friend. Diana kept a small studio in the city and maintained an active loyalty toward those galleries which had shown her paintings.

Of course, Diana could not see the plant as Justine did. Diana preferred the Italian Quattrocento Florentines: the Massaccio grandeur, the faultless Brunelleschi perspective, while Justine was far more moved by the Eychian imagination expressed in hands and faces, in detail, light and color, and by the profound van der Weyden emotion. Diana argued for della Franesca's altarpieces over van Eyck's infinities large and small. In this, they never came to terms.

Nor could Diana possibly have Justine's emotional set of associations with pink . . . when it lends a fleshy Renoir fulness that obscures form, or exaggerates innocence, or captures the roseate sentimentality which goes with glib colognes and those same disappointed bedroom slippers which scuffed along forever through the closets of Justine's unconscious. Diana's outlook tended more toward the sweeping fresco fulness of her first paintings. In these she already showed a genius for disciplined perspective in formal arrangement. The motion of her superhuman shapes and figures were beautifully, scientifically kinetic, all interplayed perfectly, coordinated with color values which seemed right enough, if somewhat overplayed and careful, perhaps less warm and exciting than they could be.

What a strange paradox, having to live with an oppressive gift when it comes from a friend. If Diana were not a friend, she wouldn't be stopping by, and there would be no reason to keep the shrub visible. Then again, it was possible that Justine's reaction was simply wrong, that she was behaving in a dogmatic or territorial way. At that thought she suffered a complete failure of conviction.

Diana had won. The high-strung, assuming energy of those flowers was enough to make her take a rare day off. Normally a tireless worker, she had no power to concentrate on her oils, and was sorry she'd spent the last two days doing the mindless work of stretching canvasses because help had been offered by visiting friends. Nor could she take over the sewing machine. She decided to fold up the frame and cover the swaths of cloth laid out on the drawing table, forget the commissions for quilts, spreads, and pillow throws, a pair of stage curtains and a velvet and silk inlaid jacket. She wanted to escape these occupied premises.

But most of the day was gone already, and she felt foolish being forced out of her own home. Couldn't she rely on the simple candor of friendship and just tell Diana the plant bothered her? She could point to its lack of plasticity, the fact that nothing mounts or echoes, or is changing or intermittent, that those flowers are not believable. They hold the purple color of satiety an elderly kind of fulness with no further expression to come, only to drop, finished—little blossom corpses—to lay all over the grainy oak sheen of her table. It was a simple aesthetic misunderstanding which could happen to anyone. But to refuse a gift from a friend. Yet, gifts, unless they were exactly right, robbed the receiver of choice. And she could never explain to Diana why she couldn't allow the plant in her home now.

She'd been honest about many differences with Diana. There were also the arguments they had always avoided, the one about pedigreed animals, for instance, though it was obvious, but never mentioned, that Sky was forced to wait outside Diana's door for Justine, even in the most miserable weather, and that Justine barely acknowledged Diana's sleek Abyssinian cat. Or Diana's admiration of European antiques vs. Justine's strict preference for American. The gold chain, another present from Diana, had come out of a fair compromise of attitude after a long discussion in which Justine admitted to avoidance of ostentatious jewelry, and it had for the moment seemed that a harmless, thin, gold trickle over her collarbones would be a pleasant break with a certainly stringent personal tradition. She wore it for a month, but lost it swimming.

What a mistake this gift was. The hideous organs peered into her sewing closet as Justine placed rolls of muslin, wool and flannel linings on the shelves, put into pigeonholes according to color those vintage cotton and chintz cut-outs from thrift shop clothing which her apprentice had purchased at the beginning of the week. She gathered up the carpenter's glue and tracing wheel, the seam ripper, razor blades and templates, set spools of linen thread on pegs and closed up the sewing chest.

She gazed across the spread of alfalfa through the kitchen window. She had made something resembling a woven tapestry using over two-thousand delicate pieces of cotton with simple embroidery stem and chain stitches to emphasize detail, and herringbones to merge the pattern into the background. It lay inert and surreal with its superb look of endurance, clinging to the empty bed upstairs. All the house's windows framed selections of local terrain viewed from within as reliable laps of nature. She had done paintings inspired by each window setting in selected light of days and seasons. The ferns and mosses pressing themselves darkly against the low glass corner of the back living room wall were done in a small depiction of enamel silken shades of terrarium green and moist black. She hung it beside the original view against the glass. The shock dawned slowly upon anyone sitting in the room. She'd done the same with another window. The far-reaching view from the sewing room included a scrap of mountain and waterfall, a shimmer of the coppery spread of decaying leaves rising up the hillside and tipping the branches in early twilight. Justine never planned her works. They were exercises of discovery. She could never work in Diana's calculated way, however much she admired it and tried.

Diana had managed to cut right into her firmest biases. It is so pragmatically unworkable to assault someone's biases. To inflict Justine with exquisiteness was to ignore her whole preference for homely, natural expression; to suggest high, finished beauty to someone who insists on a more simple, naive effect; or to foist staged theatricality on one who enjoys the innocent, accidental wildlife spectacle. The flowers seemed fixed in their pitch of ripeness which gave them an unbearable nowness. Everything else in the room showed a mutability, a scale over which the light played. The wide-plank, yellow pine floor, the warm, Low Country peasant tones of blue and brown in the rug, were continually modulated and weathered through the tumble of hours and days.

Of course, the gift could have been in answer to Justine's lack of reaction to Diana's last show. After the paintings had been so well-received: their auditory presence lauded, the setting up and cancellation of space noted, pigments judged a perfection of Nature's palette—Justine had been floored by the pure abstraction in monochrome primaries in which surface episode was almost impossible to see. Each painting was a single color field in which varying textures framed geometric shapes which appeared and disappeared depending upon the viewer's distance from the painting. There were boxes, windows and open doorways which captured the viewer at the center of the picture plane, while from other positions, the hard-edged forms jutted away from the wall. But if one stood facing the painting squarely at a medium distance, the painting did nothing at all.

Justice had greeted Diana there with relief that she had not stumbled into the wrong show. Then she blurted out with all her intensity and lack of tact: "What kind of inventions are these? They have none of your subtlety or vivacity, Diana. These masses of bottle green, untempered cadmium, lacking both representation an expression . . . ." She had hugged her friend as if soothing a child. "When did you become so removed and academic, so impersonal in your art?" But Diana's eyes held an intimidating clarity that day, in which she astonishingly resembled Leonardo's St. Anne in cartoon beckoning from a more knowing place, and Justine said nothing more.

She had not said that she actually recoiled from Diana's anti-compositions, industrial surfaces which reminded her of the hopeless painted plaster corridors inside tenements downwind of the old paper mill, where the lakes were full of careless murk and smokestacks charged into the sky. Diana had experienced enough falling out with her own peculiar childhood among weary and degenerate bohemian artists; and, now that Justine's journey had come so far, she simply never alluded to her own mother's thin-willed view of life. Riding home, after Diana's show, Justine had only complained about the soot, the traffic, the noise, the affectations and image-consciousness that arose from the constrained, artificial life of cities. She peeled and cut up raw kohlrabi she had brought from her garden with a flat, silver Swiss pen-knife, but Diana didn't want any. The sound of her own boisterous chewing filled the '65 Volvo, and hearing that, she suddenly felt the depth and breadth of her tirade. She had not meant to be insufferable.

Moved to a compensating act of tolerance when she arrived home, she ran upstairs and liberated Zack's television from the bedroom closet. After all that time she'd insisted he keep it there, that he put it away after every use, it was a telling remark that he left it. Her narrow face looked sorrowful reflected there on that blank, glassy screen, a metallic-looking sorrow of the skin as much as the eyes. She was surprised at that sight of herself, fixed in the foreground from which everything else fell away. Suddenly, looking out from that place she felt the frailty caused by chance in anyone's life and understood what Diana tried to avoid. As if Justine's being were somehow here confirmed, she wanted to treat the little box kindly because that sight of herself made it hopelessly apparent that she was too difficult to love. One is not the subject of one's world, only its clear, transmitting center.

It was a funny irony that in all Justine's works Diana had found some slight fault in her perspective. It was true. Justine had an acute eye for spatial relations and a dexterous hand. She placed things as she saw them and arrived in the end at a seemingly intended total conception. Diana, whose mother had been a sculptor, worked in exactly the opposite direction. But Diana's latest works seemed contrived. Her art was forced and untrue. A friend should simply tell her. Personal expression was nowhere to be found, her hues should have been more on the order of Venetian sensuality, of Titian or Giorgione, not so hermetic and austere. Diana had been misled into some failure of connection with herself.

Diana was a woman who thought yellow was a happy color, while Justine had to forever temper the overbearing light. The calm agreeable beauty of the countryside was just enough for Justine; the real, compelling indigo distance of the hills reminiscent of the Limbourg chapter of art traveling to Antwerp. Nature's shades held a clangorous subtlety, that was never primary or menacing, but required the beholder's constancy. Justine's own motifs were abstractions of that pure sense of countryside. Some of her most compelling mountains bore the intricate design of a moth or butterfly wing.

Maybe the answer was simple. She should return the gift to Diana. Justine could appreciate how difficult gifts really were. But everything about herself signaled discouragement of giving: that clear sense of her own hyper-response to things, her special relationship to objects despite which she had gained the love of a small group of friends and even children who particularly liked her natural way of speaking her mind. She was outright, not afraid to eat first, to laugh when something struck her, or to walk away from boors. Diana herself had pointed out that many people admired these qualities. Yes, Justine received a certain kind of admiration and liking. But never gifts.

Sometimes her mother did send some disappointing Sears and Roebuck sweater or robe, something intended to keep her warm, which of course she wore, but with a downcast air of complaint. Then last weekend Zack had sent the fishing pole, a fiberglass rod to replace her splitting bamboo pole. She had spent every twilight since Saturday beside the stream, dragging up mud and leaves, and over that course, a handful of brown trout. The pole was mounted in the mudroom they had built when reconstructing their home together. She liked the pole: one simple modern line on the spare wooden wall. The pole was meaningfully functional, reliably menial. It reflected his knowing her.

Anyone who knew her saw the things she despised: formality, urbanism, narcissism. Those flowers had them all. Opulent in a regal way that offended her own democratic temperament. Cold in their livid undertone which made them so violently objective. They were an urban conception: jarring, overdone, relentless, and alarmingly controlled, but not peaceful. Warlike. And intrusive, like blind, egocentric shouting. They were certainly not something that just comfortably hangs around the house being there as she liked things to do.

Returning the gift would be the act of friendship. It was her own property to give back. Diana had made it so. Before the plant had arrived yesterday, Justine had spent all afternoon outside splitting maple with the broad axe: a recent, practiced art in which she felt pride and freedom and the clean efficiency of muscle. After a quick shower, pleased by the economy of wood, she was speechless when Diana entered with the plant. By just walking in and placing it in the middle of the table last night, Diana had, with much fanfare, made the plant entirely, solely hers. It was hard to believe it was hers; there were so few things she actually allowed to become hers. But she was as alone in its ownership as in death.

Crossing the backyard, the blossoms trembled so that she could hardly hold the pot, and she considered going back for a shopping bag, but she did not really want to add injury by returning it in a bag. A tiny garter snake fled from beneath her oncoming sandal. She enjoyed the verdure of her lush, dappled glade which was darker, softer, more dewy than that of Diana's yard just across the stream. Diana's yard was less vivid, spoiled by dust from Route 7, neglected and dry like a bristly August meadow buzzing with flies. But it was Diana's yard Justine sketched and colored; she loved Diana's dandelions; those flowers made her smile. Diana took them for granted, thought nothing of them at all.

Justine headed for the arched, wooden bridge. A duck with seven ducklings was swimming past downstream. She looked anxiously for Sky, hoping he had not picked up their scent. These ducks were strangers who had not received the word.

The stream flowed west toward a beginning sunset which over uncounted minutes, gained a positively Rubenesque fluency and fire; such fervor raised her fear again about being Ruskin's "wrong perceiver" who vests an object with passions of his own, and makes it something it is not. But, of course, she had done exactly that. Her perceptions, like her art, were, to a fault, entirely personal.

As the earliest evening star rose above the footbridge, Justine's attention was drawn to the house of Irma Durkee across the road from Diana. there had been some movement, a curtain in a window. Then, suddenly, there was Irma out on her front porch, a long retired piano teacher, often seen watering the religious statues stationed all over her yard, or shouting at passersby. Like the voice of an oracle she called to Justine who at the same moment realized Sky was following shadowlike.

"Where are your children?" Irma implored. "You love dogs more than children," and like a madwoman Irma Durkee repeated herself in a kind of cumulative chant about dogs versus children until Justine found herself clutching the plant close to herself with an inexplicable begrudging tenderness.

'Where are my children?' she dared the thought. 'Thanks for reminding me.'

Silence followed. No cars passed, and the twilight surrounding Diana's house was drenched with the receding sunset.

As Justine approached the vegetable garden, there was the sound of a hand tool digging among soil and rock. Suddenly Diana was there, bent over with her back to Justine pulling up beets the size of baseballs. She was a large woman in sandals wearing a full gypsy-looking skirt, and a kerchief tied at the back of her neck held her long hair. That sight of Diana was overwhelming. Millet cold not have placed someone in more compelling peasant posture, or more close to the earth. Diana's rump in such direct line of vision looked enormous, skirted with the fulness of a tilted bell. Diana had spoken many times about preferring not to work in the garden in full daylight because she lived by the road and hated bending over to be seen without knowing. This stealth view of Diana caused such a sudden charitableness that Justine simply stopped to regard her friend through those huge fuchsia blossoms which themselves resembled skirts sprouting from corseted waists.

The flowers were Diana's creation in a sense, and, standing in her garden unaware of anything else, Diana seemed lovingly created by someone too. Justine was simply stationary for this single moment in which she, herself, either did or did not exist, and Sky was seated, spellbound; his tongue hung without panting and his eyes stared through the jungle of overhung hair sprouting from his forehead.

They walked home in silence.

Irma Durkee smoked a cigarette and paced her porch watching out for someone to come along. But their little procession:

woman, plant and dog moved dwarfed and undisturbed, cloaked by the Grunewaldian darkness quietly spreading among the trees.

———————

Published in *The Literary Review.* Volume 25. Number 1. Fall 1981.

The Macaw

ALONE ON SUNDAY MORNING, MERCEDES entered the shadowed corner of the zoo, her thin, floral tunic emblazoning the air like a banner. The lions yawned in their bricked enclosure, and the sun struggled to be seen above the roof. The actress planted herself within breathing distance of the lethargic lions and drew her lips back from her teeth to demonstrate the strength of hunger, as if they didn't know. The lions, in turn, searched her face with sincere, dumbfounded appetites. But it was not the lions she had come here to confront. All the lions together could not sufficiently punish the beast of rabid ambition that had rescued her from the arms of honest life.

She walked past the lions toward the birdhouse, her ancient high school sneakers silently fuming against the tarred surface. The Weekend Section had announced the return of the birds from their winter station. In the lemon-white, watery light of spring, she walked quickly, bearing travesty in her eyes. She had been alone since February. Her lover was gone, and she had given her loyal parrot to the zoo. Now inside the flight cage this moment was clear and tranquil, knitted with the soaring presence of birds. It was hard to believe that her orphaned Creon was forever imprisoned here.

Housed within the aviary was the small pavilion in which her forsaken macaw perched flightless behind wire. She had had to separate herself from him, her oldest confidant, in order to love like a normal woman. But the starved face of egocentricity had gradually returned to her morning mirror just the same, and she had painted it over with "matte and creme" to no avail. Humbled by the guilt of her lover's accusation, she had witnessed the hard, canine intensity beginning to show in her nervous jaw, and felt the spiny, grasping posture by which she had so liberally alienated him, the anthropologist, who had upset her stagecraft by casting her in the fixed limelight of love.

As she approached, the great blue Creon halted on his perch, and he fetched her real face feature by feature into one knowing eye, undeceived by the wan Ophelia despair of her manner. Except for the bite of her eyes, she had adopted a pale, protective coloring, a means of camouflaging future susceptibility to men. But the bird recognized his former owner. He expanded his golden chest and jabbered in his old noisy, dedicated way. His plumage ruffled effusively as if he was beside her at the Steinway. His reclaiming eye confirmed that somehow, still within herself, the common denominator remained. The real change was that finally she was alone, cold and firmly jelled within a roaming walrus mass of perfect aloneness, the kind one must feel at the point of dying.

Even if she could die, the bird could not be released because she had signed a contract during that time when the man made her happy. That signature survived everything, the demise of her art and the divorce of her human soul from another. All that survived of herself was vanity, without the tinge of imagination, the heart sunk in failed romance.

Creon continued looking at his original owner with one spiraling eye and then the other. During this reunion after the months gone by, two children wearing long braids entered the pavilion and were stunned and thrilled by the bird. His eyes linked with theirs, and he jumped in acrobatic friendliness with feet held to the perch—an openness the woman had always admired, as consistent as his loyalty. She hung back against the wall to watch her friend surrender and dissolve in the attention. He had an actor's perfect presence, as unstriving as that of a shapely cloud. The bird throbbed with enthusiasm among the bright children. As a ghost looking on, the woman acutely felt the unity of living things. Her knees wavered and her heart skittered and hopped with surprise.

The girls crowded together in one spot before the bird. The older one acted as emissary, flashing a toy jewel ring in the light as if Creon possessed unusual powers, and prisms of wishes fluttered everywhere in expression of the desire to remain forever whole, at the beginning of things, never to enter the great chopping blades of choice that shred and mince and parcel the adult soul. So far, the children knew nothing of that narrowing passage along which one loses options and becomes grotesquely defined. Suddenly a chain saw started up limbing a felled tree near the seal pond. Mercedes grabbed her chest for something loose within.

She felt pressure against her heels, not of the concrete floor, but of the Peruvian flat-weave rug, the anthropologist's gift, on which she had stood admitting helplessness in February. The heels and balls of her feet had burned against the figure of a woven Indian and puma fused as one, the animal molded to the human head like hair. The man had shattered his cup against the table, while she stood explaining in the warm winter breeze by the open window that her normally ascendant imagination had been flattened by contentment. Thirty times over she'd repeated the part of the miner's wife, then changed parts again, and then left the workshop to sort out her personal life, which had begun to imprison her fragile artistry. She could not afford to be lulled by personal life, she was saying when the cup exploded. Then the man was gone. Everything had stopped except the breeze from the window and the condensed vapor of boiled coffee running in streams down the insides of the clear pyrex pot. Her feet still burned with a tenderness that had persisted so long after her lover was gone.

The children seemed to enact the sharpening of morning. The sun still existed. A cloud moved and colors began. Creon's voice arose from his daring blue. "*Mal fichu*," he said. The accusation of ugliness, withheld by Mercedes's mother when she was young, had been delivered, disguised in French, by a tactless friend. She had taught the words to Creon that he might keep the swan from forgetting. Mercedes should have answered with something hateful and therapeutic. But she stayed silent there, merged with the entire gilded picture of the hopeful, sweet-voiced children and the cerulean bird.

Irony had tampered with everything. She stood violated by life, a woman alone, vestigial artist, devastated by the absence of a man she hardly knew, and robbed of the essential familiarity provided since she was sixteen by Creon: the gift she received for her unique and precocious performance of Antigone.

She was offended by the gluttonous nature of love. All that persisted was the man's wish made in thin air, that the bird be gone from her studio because of allergies and animal antipathy, because of fear caused by vanity and even jealousy of her original companion, because the man wanted her separate from her deepest attachments. He wanted to know nothing of her past. The empty coffeepot contained a permanent rainfall within her memory.

She had wanted some companionship, but both of them had tried to avoid the inevitable deepening. He talked about California when he was here in the East. At the same time, she guarded all those perfected parts of herself that were forever the blind lady stuck laughing, someone drowning, a crone too arthritic to move. Their last weeks together had passed as wine-drenched conversations over forgotten nights. But then, on top of the disappointment that their two resistant personalities could not be maintained together, she had confronted caged reality when she found that one cannot retrieve an animal given up to the zoo. Human bonds could easily be dismantled; the bird's consignment had proven the lasting thing. Consulting the curator of birds, she had simply been told that within his new habitat the bird might be encouraged to reproduce. She waited there with little wings of misery planted on her forehead.

The bird bowed toward that spot on her forehead several times, not to horrify her by demonstrating the wish to escape, but to sing his articulate miaow in a seal-point Siamese wail, a perfect tomcat howl. Her eyes turned suddenly merry, delighting in her gaudy performer, at what he had chosen of his own experience to perfect. When she had despaired of ever reconciling Creon's presence with that of her friend, she had tried other courses. Before resorting to the zoo, she had boarded him with a cat owner for as many weeks as the favor could last.

The caterwauling was Creon's poignant song of displacement. He looked roughed up, but not gloomy, and Mercedes had come to the zoo to endure with him the commitment she had put into writing, against which she could not rebel or impose her will. Alone, at last, one is free to invite anything new to happen, but seldom able to break out of old jails. The bird held the perch with claws curled toward himself, his wise and trusting face like that of childhood riveted to the woman like the reflection of her own lost instinct.

Neither one said anything. (If she had spoken, she would have cursed the contract that bound them apart, or she would have made preverbal sounds, a personal repertoire of grunts, squeaks, and jabbers that had once made her ugly, that she never truly learned to censor because those sounds felt real.) But something unseen had surfaced between the woman and the bird.

One has to admit everything. The bird had been her constant power behind the scenes, witness to her lone soliloquies before the mirror as she sketched some Desdemona, Eurydice, or madwoman onto her face. He had always listened, holding her with his tenacious gaze.

Outside for a moment in the air, she faced the vast elephant of pain, and then the focused little snout of the water shrew was blindly biting and tearing inside her like a carnivorous dream. She grasped the bars of the zebra's cage and tried to melt them. Holding to the nerves of that cage, she felt herself trapped outside the script of her making, meek and furious as the mad March hare. The one time she had not rebelled against making choices, she had inexplicably renounced everything. Now she would gladly assume any other creature's place. She would happily take the role of the hippopotamus with eyes rising out of a safely stagnant mire.

The reality she had trusted hunched up its back one day and dumped her unprepared into another cage of feeling, less friendly but more true.

In the sunny courtyard, a clown with a murderous manner pumped long, thin, colored balloons full of helium, and twisted and knotted them together into shapes of buoyant monkeys, tortoises, and bears for children standing by. The girls with long braids made pinched faces in the sun. The giraffe watched impartially; and the llama's preposterous agate gaze passed through chalky eyelashes, the parched and spitting llama, nasty from the mountain dust. All around, the complete, independent ivy raised itself over the top of the wall, teeming green over its stone partner while tortuous roots interlaced underground.

She embraced her own ribs, cradling the heavy, blue-black hollow within, tired of the weight of emptiness. The balloons were bunched together in bumping commotion, and children carried them away. The girls brought Creon a bouncing blue parrot and fastened its string to the wire lattice. Creon hollered at his likeness as if it bore some immense message. The girls yanked the string to mimic Creon's bobbing. Then, pricked by a sharp fragment of wire, the pumped-up contour popped and disappeared; a blue rubber flap was cast to the floor. Mercedes was surprised. Emptied of everything, like herself, the shape had actually failed to exist.

"Creatures beneath the sunlight are always being completed by something," she explained outside to the paired starlings lining the fountain in spring. A vacated triton, she thought, can expect a rush of surf to swarm in, a wayfaring crab to take possession.

Her shadow crossed the tar and bent head-first up the fountain steps. She turned the mute barrel of herself toward the animals, and the animals amassed. They marched toward her, and then through her, a bright procession of forms sweeping along the path that divided her. The crude piping of the elephant soothed, and the stealthy flanks of the leopard collided with the gentle sureness of the gazelle. The mother sea lion hobbled barking, her flesh sloping compliantly toward the earth. Mercedes absorbed the sullen stamp and thud of the beasts. That herd trampled her to life, until she felt thoroughly tropical, full of crawling and dripping vegetation, involuntary purple and vermilion. It was spring, and the throb of senses played. With the right faith, she thought, one can be left holding the ideal of what has been loved and gone.

Now, fixed in individual life, ready to meet the stone moment of death, when the sun no longer does anything, she loved the animals. Each one came alone. The large, sleek cats padded along, single-file, with claws retracted. They brushed through the groves of wrecked identity crowding her with their warm, assuring animal humidity. Looking over the shape of the now unclenched past, she was both consoled and bereft to find there was not a moment she would want to die in. "I also like pastel men," she said convincingly to the sloth, "who don't annihilate the private beasts of others."

Inside again, studying her old friend's face, she forgot how to speak, and instead produced something wrapped in cellophane from her Spanish leather saddlebag: overripe banana and peanut butter spread between pieces of tough rye. Mercedes stared trans-fixed as the bird held the food first in one claw, then the other, and slowly, with shared concentration, ate in his same neat way. Dwelling happily on the bird's screaming plumage, Mercedes imagined that those colors were what made him the valuable actor of this permanent tableau, the promise of splendid progeny.

No sound was uttered in the grace of their unsentimental meeting. All in secret bloom now, except for one imprisoned spot never to be touched again, she had regained the beauty by which she would be lured into the rest of her life, possessing not a single thing. The air surrounding them was shaped by acceptance, as if they allowed a kind of courtesy toward something in free flight.

Published in PERSEA 3 *An International Review.*

Published by Persea Books, Inc., 1982.

The Music Collection

YEARS LATER, FINALLY TIRED OF THE baroque pattern of moods, she was glad to have become a music teacher because of her temperament and the freedom of summers.

Survival ended the illusions of life. Many things could not be done, and some things could be done after all. Home was secured by calm porch railings, ensconced among fragrant leaf shadows spotted with light. She had earned a place up from under the deep subterranean illness of a family pinned helplessly like hidden mushrooms under the rocks, skin white as wax, hoping for those small Catholic miracles, "when there have always been politics," she said to her mother, and her mother's eyes snapped swiftly shut over the blank, dried wells of chronic insistence: "I prefer leading the choir. Politics has no love."

So many years were committed to chastity and ignorance wrapped up in itself, nervous with prayer. The choirgirls liked praying because of the beauty of churches, and of themselves dressed up, even if recognition was conferred by an invisible presence deep within a hushed, curtained tabernacle.

The years, enumerated bead by blessed bead, might have run out before the finish of the rosary. Religion would have won. The closed circle would never have permitted passing outside.

Her father's chicken revealed the way, that holy day of obligation, by plucking up and swallowing the whole fallen rosary lying in the hardened brown mud of the front path. On each bead she counted her past and future years taken up by the determined chicken's beak. While the last *Agnus Dei* still echoed, the prayer beads had trickled through the hole in her pocket, and she recognized at once the martyr and the truth.

Faith lifted its murky web then, and her latent instincts responded like once trampled flowers raising their inquisitive heads. Each morning of that summer she rowed out to the middle of the reservoir to gain unhindered perspective. The world reached beyond the vast water.

The chicken died laden with the linked jewels of her misunderstanding, its blessed little belly swollen by sacrilegious doubt. She rowed, the next morning, to the midpoint among surrounding mountains where the water rose in vapors, breathed by the spirit of early sun. Without thought, beyond the duckweed, the small wooden boat idled, the center of morning. Her fingers dangled in the still water, beneath which fish groaned from the depths. Whole vacated towns existed below, so many people had been displaced by the filling of the reservoir. One could dive forty feet to touch the steeple of an old stone church. Unaware, she drifted, without knowing that her lips moved, uttering songs as naturally as breath.

The tight, cloistered years had comprised youth, pent up now, unlived. Those years had not passed like ordinary time, but had tunneled convolutedly inside, so that something lived latent and primordial beside some internal mechanism like a clock that caused her to drop and mumble in the changed direction of the sun.

The chicken was buried out behind the garage, lying on its back with feet straight up because it sprung insistently to that position. In time the mud heaved around it, and the neighbor's rusted car parts slid on to that heroic resting spot where she had stood that day, consoling her father humbled beyond prayer by the demise of the adored chicken.

Drifting on water was a kind of sleep, the basking of a strong, hollow soul still insatiable.

HER FATHER HAD SO LOVED THE chicken because of the character it demonstrated, the flood of will; not the day of the prayer beads, but long before that, on the day originally appointed for its death. It had escaped from her mother just as the cleaver was to fall mercilessly across its neck stretched on the stump.

It got into the house, and fluttered frantically against the screens, rousing her father from the lumpy cushions of the couch which were permanently imprinted with his shape. The chicken, recognizing empathy, alighted on the rocking chair, hopping and squawking, narrowly escaping her mother's hand again as it leaped to the top of the television, pleading before the molded plaster folds of the Blessed Virgin's robes which spread to surround an abdominal clock face. Then the chicken danced under the table, and the father cried out with pain at the pathetic scratching of the chicken's claws against the linoleum. Finally it dashed up over the arm of the couch across the baffled man sitting wide-eyed. There, beside him, the chicken squatted and dropped an egg like a holy message.

"This chicken does not believe it's A chicken," her father stood and commanded silence. "The chicken is an original. This chicken is a saint!" And the chicken's life was reverently spared until the day the fateful chain of prayer beads strangled it from within. The church refused Baptism and Extreme Unction, and in a state of bitter confusion, the man threw his St. Ignatius Loyola medal and scapular into the open grave.

The next day commemorated Sainte Jacqueline, the Algonquin, whose ascending burnt sienna eyes were full of the compassion of her three-hundred years. She was the Jacqueline of weary elation; her long and legendary childhood finished, standing in the strong, agile posture of someone extending welcome, and about her the fragrance of holy water. Her legend embodied all the agonies of the little town where puddles spread slow and dreamlike, accumulated sunlight and dried. Jacqueline was simply someone thought to have existed, endowed with flawless face and other fitting qualities invented by her following.

FIRST THING THAT MORNING THE GIRL had flown forever from the farm house to the top of the hill where a network of final clawprints surrounded the springbox trickling like eternity even in the height of summer. Halted momentously on the path, she set down her baggage and gathered the full taste of pity of the day before. She saw the sunrise topping the horizon, and in a rush of tender enthusiasm perceived herself vested with that feathered little soul. Her hair fell exhausted and spread like sweaty vegetation around her shoulders. Everywhere the mountains rose in pagan spires outlining the whole vast valley of water.

Perfect silence reigned until a rooster's plaintive crowing caused a lonely fright because it seemed the crowing could not end except by loss among wind and water.

But the rare love of Jacqueline welled like a perpetual promise, encrypted and torch-lit among the marble walls, it flowered in the dim, translated glow of parishioners' faces. To them the many aunts and cousins, was given the centuries' selfless art, the splendor of stained glass and primary relics: the hair, the fingernails, the patch of prayer blanket embedded in the altar stone. The cathedral furnished them with a touch of hand-wrought beauty, for they could not otherwise imagine the nature of peace.

THE GIRL SET OUT IN THE ROWBOAT across the uncomplaining lake where she could finally face the mountainside, with the herd of stores and diners and shoe factories assembled in clapboard on the slope. Among them all Jacqueline stood, a raw soul, before the church on her day, wearing stone robes. Timeless conviction was fixed in silence between her sweeping lips.

Behind the statue, rising to the top of the mountain, leaned the tombstones of French Hill. The saint's feet were riveted in contemplation among weeds and the ancestors sleeping in the sun. At noon a gathering sat facing her with lunchboxes along the low stone wall. The saint lived independently of her followers, a mere poor girl, a fisherman's squaw. Someone set her stage. Someone erected her flesh to local fame. Requiring no confirmation of her fantastic being, she reveled in permanent silence, because she had nothing to tell, or she was not saying. Her purple gaze simply rested on that something impalpable before her eyes. She felt no regret about her audience leaving; but her audience never thought of going, they perceived only their permanent setting.

The grassy slope was riddled with places earned by families who had drifted generations ago across the border. Two-hundred-year-old veteran war medals were planted all along the proud rows, the epitaphs in the original, retained language which was now a language entirely their own, for they never adopted new ways, but they had invisibly lost touch with the old.

HOLDING THE BAGGAGE AGAINST HER knees in the boat, the girl remembered herself on other occasions. Forever gone were her days among the French schoolgirls, assembled like troubadors in the halls of the valley wine cellars, dazzling the people with bouquets of vocal harmony. Once with them in the cathedral, bearing candles in the Eucharist procession, she thought she saw in an instant Jacqueline's eye catch a glimpse of itself in the bishop's passing mirror. But she was wrong. A statue is most certainly blind.

The nuns had been overbearing that day, and it was not a mirror, but the Host itself captured behind glass at the center of the bishop's staff bearing golden rays.

Then, forgetting that the cupbearer was not to drink the wine, she emptied the goblet in one hasty draught. Moisture from her fingers spread over the altar rail where she knelt to keep from falling. Hundreds of echoing footsteps crescendoed and sighed like voices reaching through centuries. The bishop's hand was cupped lovingly under her chin, his eyes upon her grape-stained mouth. The bishop had a woman's hand. His gilded satin blurred and feathered in the candle flames, and angels came bearing down as if the ceiling had awakened. She thought the wafer waited. But instead the bishop dipped her thumbs in ink and pressed them on the empty page. He walked off sighing, proudly leafing through his book. Her lips were parted, her tongue extended. She blushed and felt suddenly protected by her skirt.

The boat seemed unable to proceed, after all the time she had been ready. Rapids had been gushing in her stifled veins so long, and then with energy derived from that dear departed spirit, the oars worked vigorously, but the boat only fluttered on the ripples. Perhaps there is no ending of the saint's long dream, protected by anonymity like her ceaseless clan. Jacqueline had merely been a local, after all, wrapped in woolen prayer blanket, a huntress with birchbark nipples, grateful to the Jesuits who were people without cruelty, unlike any others she had known. But she was not canonized. The existence of her statue attested only to a certain sore spot of rebellion and stubborn invention among the builders of her legend.

The girl had long-since outgrown her small script by studying and accomplishing her aria. Yet, for so long thereafter the boat remained riveted to the lake. The quiet water resembled the saint's gaze from the distant mountain, never shaping mind or voice. The weeds growing about the statue's feet gave

Jacqueline an air of bending. But the girl knew better than to rely on vision. The saint would not release her. She stood up in the boat to speak.

"How, with your mysterious selfishness did you attain your local beatification, saving no one else by your grasping will of the downtrodden? That you appear so kind and neutral, casting your elegant shadow over all whom you condemn is due to an exotic wiliness. But I have respected you more than all the fools since the day you apprehended my sooty little kite and returned me on my bicycle to God crouched among the grapevines growing all over my bedroom window." She remembered God's green tendrils stinging with sunlight spreading ripe, viney shadows all over the bed and chair.

IN THAT SPOKEN MOMENT THE BOAT was raided by an abrupt gust which ransacked the baggage and scattered the sheet music over the lake. Cleansed of the future, the present was no different from the lake, and the past was just a vale of childhood.

"I did not know what I would become then, simply practicing my voice with the greedy sense of promise, and weeping until sleep clouded out those mean Sundays. Imagine how this will all seem later, in live clubs, and in all those television and radio places."

In the meantime, so much time was spent handling the compass, pressing through the uncertain water toward merely another mountain only to perceive the mysterious anchor, and wonder what clues exist to explain a person remaining in a place so long. While Jacqueline with those moods of the ages smiled like the rocks, even after mounting the hillside like a speck to pray at the hem of her own woolen prayer blanket.

"Perhaps all you dwell upon, the lake before you, is the quiet welling of your sadness. But why should the lake hear you better because you had no other world?"

WHEN THE DEPARTURE IS COMPLETE, it seems that a daughter finally ceases to exist in the cradle of her past. Even if she could never really escape the barnyard, neither could she ever precisely return. The barnyard within is portable, and subject to the change of mood, and plays a tireless inner song.

But the beauty of the region lays inescapable claim upon the natives. They have their niches in the mountains from which to lay hold of the young. It could have been predicted that she would wake up there again one morning in another June, in a fine old house, so far from her last performance in the concert hall. A husband too, still in full-costume, would have come to touch this peace established among tribulation.

The mountains, from the other side, have come to represent the never-ending wish. Others like themselves have escaped there before into those magnificent abandoned houses deep in the woods, out of the reach of local memory or roads grown over. The outsiders come and go without anyone knowing, except perhaps the local students who seek them out. The mountains shield anyone.

At first they marvel how everything shows itself new in the sunlight. They rest their voices, their violins. They live among the dew and raspberries, not without knowing. They arrest a daring happiness. The house exists among meadows and trees overlooking the lake of learning. Speechless and listening they sit up together in the dawn and comprehend vitality.

JUST WHEN THEY WERE CERTAIN THAT no one would ever find them, a new chicken appeared like a miracle on the lawn, arrived as if by intention, clucking along the railroad track, so sure of itself, pecking its way out of the mist.

The chicken was a frantic and bloodthirsty lunatic who subdued the husband and injured his ankle. The dog skulked off to the forest with a wounded haunch. No young people arrived for music lessons after that. The girl stood helplessly by the window with the metronome, while the chicken started at sunrise parading back and forth outside, bristling with arrogant feathers.

The couple disagreed about the chicken. Each daybreak the young man was at the washbasin recounting how the chicken was a riddle sent to live among them for a while. The girl despised local riddles, and said that the weak were always out to arrest the strong. She maintained that her generosity was in shreds. But he saw something sacred about the bird, and wanted to receive its inspiration. She wanted to shoot it from the music room window. Instead, the husband invited the chicken to sleep in the cat's potato sack behind the kitchen stove where he respectfully questioned the contentious little eyes blinking from the burlap swaddling in the dark.

He insisted that happenings be perceived as metaphors, reviving her past in a landslide. If the first chicken had naturally commanded the terrifying intimacy of love, he said, the second lived alone in its personal nightmare, part of the mysterious tragedy of beings. And there, as he hitched his overalls and put on his frayed straw hat before the mirror, she thought he resembled someone mesmerized by an oppressor.

Long after she felt successfully tyrannized, one day there arose from the darkened music room a sudden disruptive burst of unbearable sound which continued for long moments until she located the animal inside the upright piano roaming over the wooden hammers and plucking the strings. She cursed the beast for causing chaos and dislodged and beat it with the baton.

But the chicken could not be insulted or impressed. It sprang from the piano and strolled out on the front porch to drench itself in sunlight, and finally descended the stairs to the barnyard where, red and glowing, it paraded over the runny meadows like a Mary in oil on velvet.

When the husband in the garden spotted the chicken passing his eyes lighted with something like recognition. Something rekindled all sense of wonder and childish empathy with simple beings: the chicken going along, hopping up and down, nervous in its ways, simply life.

"Faith must be returned to," he said, leading his reluctant wife over the pliant tussocks in the direction of new longing. "Something must alter one's perceptions along the way. It hardly matters what."

And that was how the procession began. the man followed the chicken all over the fields, up the hillside, along the sky. The chicken ignored the giant shadow that moved carefully behind with the sagging knees of someone on an ancient quest. He was with utmost care approaching the most compelling mystery of religion, the mystery of love. For love was a spiritual manifestation, he said: what Christ knew, what the bible knew, and what is known by certain birds of Tibet. And love, he said, was greater than everything, greater than suffering.

And that was how the bishop himself came along. the girl was driven to writing so many letters, and the bishop had been a local boy. The bishop followed the husband, and the last time she saw them, they paraded like a managerie single-file across the sunrise, seeking to complete among themselves some common soul.

DRAWN AGAIN BY FATE, THE GIRL departed in the rowboat. There was only Jacqueline, after all, waiting like a spider by the dangerous lake, possessing her little bag of earth, and doomed to the continuous pity of her robes. The oars were splintered, dry and senile, the water old, and the rowboat tolerant of little droplets running in. The saint was worn out after the long trial and celebration that had gone on without her, and most apparent was her sorrow for ever having symbolized false love.

"Now, Jacqueline, I stand here lame with innocence, large and naked, and dying of mistakes beneath this undisclosing sky, never to forget our ignorance as children when we pelted you with pebbles. As I speak, I see that your summer smile is internal to my gesture.

"Will there be a moth ticking at the light bulb to remind me that I sleep? Or, perhaps bumping my head once has caused this flight of years. Having escaped all past description, it is you, Jacqueline, who convinces me I am really here."

At some point in time one discovers one's work in the world. Teaching in the classroom seemed quite promising after all, when one sees all their upturned little faces and understands what it is they have to learn. Music carries us forward, and their beautiful voices do go on.

———

NO PRELUDE WAS INTENDED, BUT SIMPLY, in that moment when the assembly stood and the sun increased, just as the fingers were so perfectly poised above the keys, the body capsized gracefully, slid like a gush of quicksand across the gathering which had just achieved its collective intonation. It snapped at the ankles: and the head, in profile, assumed a resting place in the lap of the nervous soprano.

Everything failed at the sight.

That was the last reunion. The chant never had a beginning. But the song continued in each voice.

———

SO MUCH LATER, SOMEONE WILL come walking here and discover in the overgrown forest, the porch with sagging railings, and weeds and young trees grown up through the floorboards. Inside, mold fills the abandoned wine glasses beside the unfinished game of chess, and the needle hovers chronically above the next note. Perhaps they had been dancing before the magnificent mirrors hung like dying actresses among the lavish lamplight. The librettos are old; the deer have eaten the fly-speckled pages; and the dinner has long-since been cleaned off the plates by the mice of winter.

That someone who comes will wonder what they had escaped here from, before ascending so hurriedly into the night.

———————

Published in *WIND* Literary Journal. Volume II–Number 40–1981.

Anticipation

THAT SUMMER STARTED OUT brilliant yellow like the dawn.

Headed to Old Orchard Beach, I talked with John Keats, in the backseat of Uncle Frannie and Aunt Jilda's car. I took Keats with me everywhere.

"You knew so well that never and forever are the same," I softly praised my poet.

"I knew what?" Aunt Jilda responded from the front seat, and turned to offer me a lemon drop from a little tin candy box. Her nails were frayed from working in her garden and from her devoted rescue of hurt and fallen birds.

"Never and forever are the same," I said.

"Well, that's what I thought when I married Frannie," she said, blowing a huge bubble with her gum, which popped. Newly married, they were both twenty-six and had dark wavy hair and freckles. "I thought it would never happen. And now here we are forever . . . . ."

"And ever and ever and ever . . . . ." Frannie chimed in from behind the wheel, leaning a smile toward his wife. But Keats understood that I was talking about the Grecian urn, where the lovers frozen in time never capture one another, never fulfill their desires, so they go on forever in the state of delicious wanting.

My thoughts that day were a poetry of my own sweetest wanting, of the lemon-rich anticipation of seeing my cousin James: of me and James at the seashore, like the Bobbsey Twins on family vacation, as we had once been. He'd be there now, waiting for me and I was reminded of all the other times I'd traveled to see him. Throughout the first decade of my life, my mother and I had visited my Aunt Dimanche, "Aunt Sunday," and her son, James, most weekdays. All the way there in Mum's car, I used to plant kisses on my own fore-arm and whisper 'James, *je t'aime* and relish the delicious nutty smell of breath on my skin.

I still felt that James and I were the only two people in the world, and all for each other. Our dance duo had stretched through all our childhood, our little *pas de deux*: swirling and tapping through many recitals; dipping and swooning, eyes locked, bodies moving together as if glued. It had all culminated in the jitterbug contest we'd won five years before, when I was eleven and he was twelve.

Then suddenly, our dancing days were over. They were done because James had pronounced them dead. Just like that! Disappointing both our mothers and me. So had ended all those years of just the two of us on a lighted small-town stage, with audiences of aunts and mothers and lipsticked smiles lavished upon us with warmest applause. So too ended our joined life, having started together as babies in the crib. My mother and Aunt Sunday lived together with Mimay (their mother) when our fathers were gone in that last year of the war.

Not long after ending our life on the stage, James stood in the mirror and grease-slicked his dark brown hair, turned up his collars, adorned himself with gold and silver chains, black loafers with white socks and peg-pants, and became: Bad! And inscrutable! He donned a permanent cigarette (no hands), his mouth a brutal slant. I did not know yet that he had dropped out of high school. I only knew he had assumed an air of danger and a wolf-like coldness and that he wore it well. He still danced with me at weddings and baptism parties, as our two mothers' younger siblings continued marrying and having children and grand little celebration parties at their modest, French-Canadian gathering club. James had developed a whole new way of moving in sudden jags, with what I thought was a thrilling but comfortable violence. I remained on the stage myself a little longer, a lone starlet, dancing the Merry Widow's Waltz for a few die-hard kind ladies. Then I quit too. Family circumstances interrupted everything and James and I nearly lost sight of each other for the next five years.

My personal vista turned to empty buckled roads run between warehouses, where daylight lay murky and pointless on the surface, or dried to dust. I more than outgrew some feverish crushes, and then began finding poetry in the cracks and crevices of my own home town in a remote part of Massachusetts, where spirits dried up and died young. Among the depressing scrapheaps, I found John Keats and made him mine: the reason he was with me on that new yellow day heading north.

Keats held one side of an ongoing argument I had with myself about growing large or staying small. Growing would mean going beyond everything I knew. And small would mean remaining cozy and comfortable in the lap of the family myopia. But with small, nothing would ever happen. Keats made all the difference in my little mill town, where people were too soon devoured by the condition of sagging small-mind, at woefully early ages. Keats held the eye of the large wide open, keeping watch with his words of magnificence and encouragement and eternal youth, as each of my friends and family fell one by one into what I called 'the glump of dull.' Other than James, Keats was my only love.

Keats's nightingale, his Grecian urn gave a sweep of time to the 'nothing happening' problem of an ordinary day. The poet had a velvet voice. He almost purred beside me. That was the beauty of having him. I could make him into anything I wanted. It was a joy to be joining my mother's sisters and brothers and their families, going to the beach with Keats. Dreams had charged the two whole days before we set out. I eagerly pictured my cousin's comic antics among the gleaming beach sand, not imagining he had changed. Keats could understand a dreamy person energizing her young life with ecstatic visions. I didn't see why my life should be without anything in it.

My Keats had Elvis-Presley eyes, with lashes so long and graceful and artistic, they looked like they should play piano. He danced in words, bequeathed his dance of language to the world. I was so glad that Keats had been born and lived, even if not in my time. Whenever I turned to him, I saw a continuation of dawn without time.

As for the rest of my life: if I didn't go to school until one, then work in the Diner 'til five, then baby sit and baby sit and baby sit—there would be no money, and frankly nothing to do. Sometimes I drove the family car around back roads, listening to rock and roll, replacing some of the words in songs with Keats's words, sometimes my own. A few friends sometimes came with me, kids who also lived on the northside of loneliness.

By sixteen, the peroxide-blonde streaks in my hair were growing out with the pace of my maturity. And the adults talked to me. I got a new respect, as if I had done something.

"So, then they found her, right where they'd never thought to look," Jilda was telling a story, "after searching all night." The conversation in the car dwelt on the reason some of the family were spending their vacation at the shore. It seemed that dear fiery Aunt Sunday had recently gone off the deep end. She got drunk at the club one night—an unusual thing for her to do. Then she disappeared. People were out looking for her until three in the morning, when Uncle Pete found her right in the big stuffed chair in the living room with a large marmalade cat in her lap, both sound asleep. This was astonishing because Sunday had a strong dislike for cats. This cat was a stranger, the exact color of Sunday's hair, as if she'd plucked it out of the mirror. No one ever knew where this creature came from. But Aunt Sunday, a tomboy all her life, had participated in a local barroom brawl, throwing punches with the men before she disappeared, got drunk and acquired a pet. The cat stayed on and reigned like a prince. So, it was decided that Aunt Sunday needed a good vacation, near the comforting prayerful relaxation of the waves. And of course, everyone would go. I was glad to be off on a journey that I was calling kismet: seeing James again.

"Loomyay," cried Jilda!

"What?"

"The cat's name. It means light." The French-Canadian family past, sifted down through several American generations and three New England states, had shaped its language with long slow change.

I went on in my state of dreaminess in the back seat, remembering the special childhood James and I had shared. That was in Mimay's, house, where Sunday and Pete, and all my mother's younger brothers and sisters remained living, even after they were married. It was a deteriorated old mansion—triple-storied, with porches spilling out atop porches and a cupola with fractured windows on top of it all. The bottom porch floors had broken and splintered floorboards, and were burdened with old stoves and washing machines no longer useful. Mimay herself lay dying in her bed on the second floor for some twenty years—leaving my mother and Sunday, when they were children, to beg for the family's food in town—and there Mimay stayed all day among her religious statues, with many pairs of rosaries looped over the four posts of her bed. Various priests paid visits to Mimay, and one of them brought her a TV one day—a new invention at the time.

"We learned to soak our bread in water," my mother told me how they survived as children and how they all had 'rickets.' "Wet bread fills your stomach better."

For James and me time was stunned still in that house. The magical spot of our childhood was the sunny upstairs "ballroom" that topped one long porch. A whole wall of windows caught the morning there. In its day, that room had hosted some little birthday parties and the long, purling flow of unchanging child-play. But its prime was over by our time, and on one of its last occasions, before James and I could walk, it had hosted a signif-icant hurricane. A large, old elm had been lifted and deposited horizontally through the roof of this surprise chamber. The tree lay supine, shapely and denuded as a muscular, young god. The faded oak floor was supported beneath by I-beams of steel which were original sections of the Eastern Railroad.

James and I walked up that northern flight of stairs, and headed left off the hall. We passed Mimay, permanently stationed in her bedroom on the right, calling out *"merde,"* and *"mange le crud"* to boxers on TV. We stepped through French doors onto a long stretch of wobbling outdoor balcony backed by lichened windowpanes, and along which bushes grew through cracks in their pots. We entered one of those windows into this magical room, where the leafless fallen tree made an incredible balance beam. There in our tap and ballet shoes, we practiced our routines. The floor echoed and the trunk made for defiant leaping points, a relief from the seriousness of our usual drills.

Not only did Mimay's house hold vast reaches, the surround-ing property had once been grand. Beyond Frannie's junked jalop-ies in the yard, with sleeping dogs hanging off the sun-warmed roofs and hoods, had been a lovely, if overgrown, garden, with walkways among robust flowering things. We were told this was our grandmother's garden, but it was impossible to imagine how.

At most, Mimay managed on rare occasions to come down into the living room and flump into the big stuffed chair by a window with a different view from her upstairs usual. But somehow, Mimay had created this garden at some point in time—and in the middle of it all stood a cluster of plaster baby angels, all looking heavenward, uttering messages we couldn't fathom.

"I have to pee," James had announced suddenly one day, dancing around like an exaggerated drunk.

"Water them," I indicated the little naked fellows with wings.

And so began a game we played, where James could christen things that I could not and it increased our merriment and our joint imagination. We had many reasons to love.

"You look like you're in your own world back there," Jilda commented as I sat in silence. She offered me another lemon drop.

"Yes," I admitted. I was besieged by fond memories all the way to the shore, barely able to contain my hope: not knowing it was headed for shipwreck. Our family's nightmares were like that: nothing jumps out in the course of things to let a person know it's time to run, or wake up, or get out of the way. I was just living my innocent excitement, imagining James reeling through his constant comedy routine of wisecracks, and Aunt Sunday, swearing and cursing with such ease, she was a poet at it. But now I had Keats, and his vision of the 'large.'

In fact, my tender anticipation had not been without doubt. The large versus small argument had been going on inside myself all the way there. While the family hearth was always warmed by jokes and laughter, it was based on a refusal to see beyond itself. Yet it was hard to resist the lure of comfort. I had been sitting on Frannie's blanket spread out on the car's backseat. The blanket had a row of Indians with orange faces, running one behind the other with tomahawks held high. I knew that blanket well and all it had been through, probably from the beginning of my life. I knew when I was six that Frannie cried on that blanket in the night, having been drafted to fight in Korea. Mimay heard him in his room in the cupola—a double flight above Mimay's room.

This was a family that never said hello or goodbye. When my mother and I had walked into Aunt Sunday's house (Mimay's house) all those long-ago weekdays, never knocking, no one looked up. No one seemed to notice we had ever left and come back. But always, when he was younger, James sat somewhere in the vicinity of our arrivals, burping or pumping his arm with the opposite hand cupped under his armpit to make sounds he called 'quackfarts.' In those wiseguy antics (he also did great Red Skelton and Jerry Lewis imitations) I recognized his happiness to see us; it was its own kind of greeting. Those were timeless, ecstatic days. The four of us walked together through town. "Hey Lard-arse," Aunt Sunday would shout out and whistle with her fingers at the corners of her mouth, to hail Uncle Frannie, whom she had spotted across the street in the middle of town. Frannie blushed all the way up his face and out to his ears, realizing everyone around had heard. James and I and my mother too, could hardly stand, we laughed so hard.

The family lived like they were all just one, with no distinctions. Even Aunt Jilda just slipped right in. No judgements. No having to please. No price of admission. Everyone was just who they were. My mother was just Aunt Helene, James's mother was just Aunt Sunday, his father just Uncle Pete; just Uncle Frannie, now just Aunt Jilda. And James was just James. The temptation was to stay in that family fold, as if Fate—if it caught you alone would take you in its teeth and shake you hard. But if Fate found everyone all stuck together, it got no place to take hold. Yet I didn't want to be 'just Lucy.' I wanted to be the one-and-only Lucy, and I thought that I would risk my own fate.

In the car, with stark farms speeding past, I was enveloped in the smell I had always known. Frannie's blanket spread out on the back seat smelled like everything in Mimay's house, a deep earthy ambience. It was the family smell. James lived in that smell and sometimes had it in his clothes, but never in his stage costumes: those zoot suits, straw hats or sailor outfits. I entered and emerged from the smell—maybe it hung on me when I was there, but not when I was not there.

I speculated about that smell with Keats, a kind of woodland creature himself. Did it come from the house or those who lived there? It hung in the draperies, got into the couches and emitted from the dark wood. The browned player-piano keys were sticky with it. Was it the smell of staying put? The Indians with raised tomahawks—on whom I sat, slightly itching my legs in short shorts—were all running in the same direction, in the manner of the figures on Keats's Urn, and would never bring their tomahawks down, would never slay one another in their Keatsian state of incompletion. Maybe it was the smell of generations, down into the shoe factories, following the paper mills, where the logs spilling down the river had Mimay leaping them as a little girl. The smell included strong stews, boiled frogs legs, cigarette smoke and homemade wine. Squirming on that prickly blanket, I felt myself transported to my next understanding of life.

I WAS SURPRISED THAT THE RENTED house in Maine resembled Mimay's own home, a heap of stories with upstairs porches hanging off.

"Son of a bitch! Look at ya, all grown up." Aunt Sunday and Uncle Pete were out waiting on the wide front porch.

"Pete, will ya look at this beautiful bombshell," she flattered and embarrassed me.

The porch embraced all four sides of the first floor. But other porches climbed the walls. There were porches to make the heart leap. Sunday stood there carrot-colored from toe to head, cursing and shouting. She was boisterous and spunky and enviably crass.

I kissed Mimay, and she pinched my cheek, thrust her lips at me, and called me '*cherie.*' I was surprised to see her out of bed—lumpy, with cumulous flesh overflowing her beach chair, each ponderous breast practically someone to be addressed. Aunt Mercredi, as usual, wore a black eye and flooded tears, safe at last, away from her brutal husband. Some younger cousins and the marmalade cat dotted the terrain. Uncle Pete came forward oozing warmth: "God luv ya," he said, as he always did, with such glad feeling, it could have been a song, and he cupped my cheeks in his shaking hands. Keats stood beside me as I hugged Aunt Sunday, who smacked me on the fanny. When I asked for James, they all grew silent and pointed out through the window to his new car: his first—parked up the sand-grass road. I saw a black '56 Chevy with yellow panels. It matched the Pez dispenser he'd chased and 'shot' me with all over the Provincetown sand dunes on the family's last vacation, a couple years before. I had retaliated with mine in pink and black. Now he owned a car, in his own Pez colors, and it was slunk in the reeds as if hiding.

I asked for James again and someone announced it was time to eat. When I turned to face the whole large room, I actually saw a black foot disappear like a stealthy varmint around the door frame. I flew after it, knowing it was James playing one of his games. But why? Then I heard voices of laughter up the stairs and movement ahead of me—running away. Something new. There were voices—and one was a girl's. I started up the stairs.

"James?" I called out, but I knew that whatever was going on was intentional.

I followed up yet another flight, down some hallways onto a screened porch on the third story looking out to sea. An outside stairway descended from this porch straight down to the beach sand. "James!" Its steps were still springing and two young people ran across the grassy beach sand away from the house. One was James, clearly holding hands with a thin girl in a mini-skirt, heading for his car. Then they started up and took off. The engine sound made the floor shudder under my feet.

"Don't worry about anything," came the voice of Keats, ready to waltz me with comforting words. "You're the best of all of them, no matter what happens." Then he and I stood together watching down on them as the car took off. All that happy hope and heartset in the backseat, heading up on the highway, now turned to gloom. I lumbered down the stairway to the large kitchen, where everyone was gathered around in the afternoon sun, and nestled my pain right into the family warmth. That warmth was presently hung with curls of sticky flypaper and the hum of captured insects sounded, buzzing to oblivion.

"You should'a seen Toohey the other day," my Aunt Sunday was telling a story as she tapped the saltshaker over her glass of beer. "He shows up. It's been raining all day and he rings the doorbell. Toohey never rings the doorbell, he's been our next-door neighbor for more than 15 years; Toohey just walks in. So, I answers the door and he's wearing a raincoat. I says, 'Toohey, what the hell?' And what's he do, he spreads his raincoat wide open and whadd'ya know, he's gut nuthin' on under there. My mouth flies open. I says, 'Toohey. You got the most warped sense of humor I've ever seen. Only you could think 'a this.' Meantime, I was standing there splitin' my sides. 'What a card (she pronounced it kaaahd),' I says. 'Toohey you get home and put your pants on before you scare the hell outa me. I don't wanna look at that thing. Only you, Toohey. I don't know how you come up with what ya do. You're a helluva clown and you go the mile. I'm gonna be tellin' this story for the rest of the week. Only Toohey. There's only one Toohey." Everyone laughed as if Toohey won the stand-up comic prize. It sounded like Toohey himself laughed all the way home. And they all went on just loving each other.

So, HERE WE ARE AGAIN IN the bliss of ignorance, I thought. No reason to bother with the real point of anything. Everyone was so complacent, good-natured, viewing everything in some perpetual dawn light, that they never had to feel disturbed, feel the pain of life, even when my uncle was a teenager crying on his Indian blanket, alone in the night. They tasted their lemons with a sweet-tooth. I had to wonder if it was this peculiar contentment that made for the family habit of long life.

Many had been comfortable into their 100-plus years in North Adams. Maybe there was wisdom in just refusing all recognition of adversity. Too late, they realize something's happened, when the water or something else is up around their ears. Then there's nothing to be done anyway, so they just relax and go along. Bail out the boat, even if it's got a hole in it. James knew he was safe in this fold forever, no matter what he did. And I had been prepared to immerse myself in the family affection and sloppy contentment just for the weekend. Until the foot flew around the corner. And the foot kept going, around every corner I turned— for the entire weekend.

Now I'D LOST MY APPETITE. All the windows were open and salty humidity and voices drifted in uttering *"mange du-tout,"* from other houses plotted in the sand. I knew without wanting to that there were better places, more beautiful beaches where people didn't litter and scream all day or make their children feel to the world like too many children. But the consolation was, if you sink to the lowest, you finally have the ground beneath you, and then you just go around content and comfortable on the basic earth.

"Happy as pigs in shit!" my mother would say.

I left a hot dog untouched on a paper plate with potato salad and pickles on the checkered oil cloth. Then with a glass of lemonade in hand, I went out on the porch, wandered around all four sides, and down the wooden stairs. Pete was at the barbecue. He gave me a plate with steaming ears of corn, which I placed with my glass on the picnic table. Then I walked along the soft road toward the blue nape of water between shoulders of sand.

I only caught one glimpse of James's girl. She was small and slim, standing on the beach for a fleeting moment—not beautiful or sexy—but rather a sensible-looking girl, with short close-cropped, hair and bangs. Keats stood beside me as we viewed her. I learned that this girl had graduated from the class James had dropped out of and that she got A's in math and already had a job as a secretary. I was stunned by a strange new person in our midst. I saw her instantly as James's life raft and a way to run from me: a relationship too intense, that had to be exploded.

THE VIEW OF THE WATER WAS comforting now. It had nothing to do with us. It was outside us. Keats and I walked and walked along the shore, watching ships and boats moving on lone courses, unlike the figures on the Grecian urn or the Indians on the blanket, none were in pursuit of the other: no love or death sought in their plying the waters. Voyagers simply going alone. Tides sweep, rise and fall. James was gone from the beach, and every time I looked, the car was gone.

The spent waves licked my feet like kitten-tongues. My bitter sadness got reeled back out to the mighty sea. I reflected mournfully, how Keats had faced his own impending death at twenty-six: "When I have fears that I may cease to be, ..." I wandered back through the poetry of his years to his young death, and pictured hunch-shouldered tombstones, tilting souls, captured in ancient moss. I felt his life in my throat when I said his words aloud: ". . . before this pen has gleaned my teeming brain." But gleaned it had. Our only mismatch was our place in time. Everything he said about himself reached deeply into me. And as I walked back to the house, I filled myself with the smell of fresh salt air.

SOMETIME DURING THE NIGHT, James and his girlfriend snuck in and moved around like mice in the walls. "Forget them," Keats assured me. "They're stupid and they don't know a good thing." I caught one more disappearing act as some living part of my cousin was snatched from my view before I could even know if it was a shoe or a pantleg or a sleeve. The vanishing dark foot was the lasting image of that weekend. James and his friend did a grand disappearing act every time I moved.

SO, THE NEXT MORNING, I WALKED on the beach alone.

My mood was so raw and purple I could not even fall into Keats's plush spell. I could not be held by his word-hands, his word-arms. Keats was in fact long owned by death and his leftover voice was that of neverending longing. I had to admit I was alone. I stood on the heightened boardwalk looking out across the water to the question of a mountain-island out in the sea, a glorious, coniferous green. What was there? As I stared, a road materialized, like a thin rubber band circling that emerald eruption in the blue. Who went on that road?

"You look like someone having a vision," said a voice suddenly, almost magically, to my right, and an intimate shadow lapped my shoulder like a slurp of low-tide. I did feel like someone having a vision.

"What?" came my answer, but I melted into this shadow, feeling an instant familiarity. Had I just created a soothing hallucination? Had I brought Keats to life, and made him flesh again in 1960?

"What are you watching out there?" Unlike my vanishing cousin, or my make-believe playmate, here was a whole person continuous with his shadow. About my own age, with a sensitive face, delicate but strong build, and hazel eyes with a violet cast. His name was Blaise Boucher, and he wore dark-rimmed glasses and looked intelligent and positively poetic. We told our reasons for being there in that same spot, in that same moment of our lives, and found that Keats was both our favorite poet. Blaise was a 'private school' student and now he was at camp on that island I had been studying and he rode his bicycle every day on that very road that looked like a rubber band.

He spoke of his Uncle Tom, who was responsible for his being in this private school, and who took him on nature journeys twice a year, and these were the high points of his life.

We walked for miles on the seashore and the best stories Blaise told were about those travels with his uncle. These were amazing stories about being far away. They went to Death Valley, the second hottest place on earth. Then once, camping in an Arizona canyon, they were alerted in the night by a gathering sound. 'Grab your things,' his uncle had said. 'It's a flash flood.' They packed up and ascended a canyon wall in minutes, then watched the furious water fly by. There were other stories about private planes in remote parts of Alaska and mapping unmapped regions, and bear scratches on someone's bald head when he woke up in the morning—but the flash flood captured my imagination most. Weren't we always having flash floods in our lives. Amidst all the calm and the sweet-okay was suddenly a reason to gather and reposition yourself. Little did Blaise imagine, I was rapidly replacing James with him—beside the unreal Keats. Suddenly Blaise had Keats's deepset eyes and passion.

Blaise and I recited Keats's poetry together and some of our own poetry too as we walked the edge of those waves. Our profound togetherness lasted that one whole day—from low tide to high.

Just as the sun moved down toward the sea, I said: "I understand Keats's wish to make time stop just before the good things actually happen—his wish to be forever in the state of anticipation. Anticipation is my favorite thing."

"But then he never gets the good thing," said Blaise, looking at me with concern.

"But then he never loses the good thing. If you get the good thing, the next thing that happens is it's gone. It's not new anymore, and maybe not so good anymore. He knew that."

"What makes you think that?"

"Well, then you get old. No one on the urn gets old—that's what he wanted. That's how I'd like my life to be."

"By nothing happening? You'll get old anyway."

"I know that . . . ," I was beginning to feel I should defend myself.

"I can't picture you old, someone who looks like you—" he grew shy—"with all that gold in your hair."

"I'm glad you think I look good."

He bought me an ice cream.

"Anyway," I said, eating for the first time since I'd arrived. "I live too much inside my head." The same was once true of Blaise.

Blaise worked in the school cafeteria—rising at 4:30 in the morning for the breakfast session. But he did the whole three meals a day and clean-up lasted late into the night. This sparked my interest. He was like me, not afraid of hard work. But in describing his studies, his Latin, his history, his advanced math and science, he was talking about a discipline of the mind I had never imagined, but decided I would take on as soon as I could and make mine forever.

My future was suddenly inspired. I couldn't wait to go back to our new guidance counsellor and revamp my last year of high school. No more shorthand, typing and bookkeeping. My next courses would be Latin, algebra, geometry and science. And I would consider further education, which had never been a thought. College was for "geniuses," my family said. But I could be like Blaise—doing well; clearly, he and I alike were on our own.

At the end of the day Blaise called me a fantastic girl and promised to dream about me, not just tonight, but every night from now on.

"Forever?" We both promised forever. And there is that part of each other still striding through our dreams.

Moments fly through the universe and never change and never end. Forever never ends. But of course, other moments follow and I would have the rest of my life in a different mold now from what it would have been if James had stayed loving me and if Blaise had not stepped in.

Actually the next morning, soles of shoes disappearing like ghost-mice again, I sought the shore and celebrated my own new being—right there under the sun.

I didn't have to remain stunned by fate and forever-after looking out to sea. I could move toward that horizon like the tide. James would just bump on that mysterious divide and get a headache. But I could dance right up and step over.

Notes

A Liberal Education

Mimay—French-Canadian for grandmother—is spelled Mémé in French. I chose to spell it this way to read more easily.

Poika: 1929

This is an extrapolation of a story my father told about something that happened in his life when he was a boy. His parents were out working and never home when he returned from school. And his home was at an under-developed end of town. He would set off into the woods. One day he discovered a body. A man who had hung himself and finally the rope had broken and let him down. Of course, this terrified a boy of eleven. I think he went to some neighbors. Then he had to wait in his own house until his father came home after dark. The true story simply didn't work. Truth is stranger than fiction. So it had to be fictionalized.

Poika means boy in Finnish. I was aware of a boy in my home town who everyone called Poika. I learned that his mother was a serious alcoholic, there was no father, and they were terribly poor. He had straight yellow hair that hung over his face. I was deeply moved by him.

Poika in the story, is, of course, my father as a boy.

Karjalainen—is based on my paternal grandfather, Oscar Lindquist. Exactly.

Aiti—means Mother. She is based on my grandmother Linda Lindquist (née Linda Kylmala Johnson), who was my caretaker when I was very young. She and my grandfather lived upstairs in our house. My paternal grandparents.

Kaukanen—is based on a man who scared me in the woods one day.

I was picking blueberries on what was un-owned land. This man was huge, frighteningly white, and probably insane. He claimed those were his blueberries, that I was on his land and he chased me.

My father was home that day and I'll always remember the scene—my tall father standing with his hands against the chest of this burly white man (his all-one color made him all the more dreadful, combined with his irrationality), who towered over him, my father calming him down.

Suvetar

Suvetar is the story of Aiti (Poika's mother) returning home for her day off.

I was much enamored of the writing of Clarice Lispector (Brazilian author) at the time I wrote this. She was my inspiration. It was meant to be Chapter 2 of Poika: 1929.

Both of my grandparents were my caretakers in my earliest years, when my parents worked by day. I knew them well.

Loyal Opposites

These characters are an amalgamation of some very interesting, brilliant, complicated people I knew in the late sixties. Their neuroses were complicated too and I wondered at the time what it must be like to be their children.

I have sisters who are identical twins (of a set of triplets). I borrowed a couple of interesting details they've shared with me.

Work on the polycarbonate house caused a severe illness in someone engaged as a helper. I no longer recall the details.

The Gift

I was with a friend in Jerusalem—the place was causing me a sacred feeling.

We sighted a hanging basket of operatic blossoms before us.

They took my breath away and I exclaimed at the plant's beauty.

"They're fuchsia," said my friend. "I hate them."

That experience gave rise to this story.

Maybe the two characters—Justine and Diana—are two sides of the same person.

I've also often pondered the nature of gifts, what they mean and don't mean—to the giver and to the receiver.

I chose a hyper-aesthetic personality, hopefully at just a moment in time. She's meant to be someone who can undergo personal evolution. I've given hints of that. She is not meant to seem too rigid.

The Music Collection

This story comes directly from the unconscious—as in a dream. I looked for the coherence afterward.

What's it about? Do I really know myself?

The editor of Wind Magazine sent me his empty lunch bag on which he spiraled in pen the opinions of his staff. They had spent a lunch hour trying to decide whether to publish the story. All of them thought it was compelling writing. All of them did not understand what it was about. Some thought the meaning should be comprehensible in order to publish. Others said the reader could decide the meaning for themselves. Ultimately, the yays had it. So it appeared in 1981.

I could venture it's about a young woman who grows up feeling surrounded by compelling beauty, in her environment and in her church.

Her music begins there.

But it's all local and she gets to the point in development of wanting to join a wider world. But her origins have a profound hold. She finds it difficult to leave (the boat can't move on the lake). She aspires to a larger beauty—both personally and spiritually.

The chicken—brash, superior innocence.

When I was four and we lived on O'Moore Avenue with my paternal grandparents, I left my Kewpie doll, Bumpsky (named by my father) in the road one day where cars almost never came. But one did. And Bumpsky lay with a crushed and broken head. My father was so upset, I found myself consoling him—not the other way around. Thus, the father lamenting the chicken in this story.

I think we took Bumpsky to a doll-hospital in Waltham and probably she got fixed. Where did Bumpsky go in all these years?

Jacqueline—cast in stone. An object of the projections of others. She thus belongs to others. What it takes to be a saint. She is the mystic, who escapes longing, the small sense of self, speech and need for moving and wandering—all those earthly leanings. She is one early ego-ideal of the story's narrator.

Anticipation

This story was written in 1971.